Showdown at Firefly Island

By Eli Clark and Gerry Boylan

Illustrations by Aaliya Davidson
aaliyadxart@gmail.com

Copyright © 2022 by Gerry Boylan

All Rights Reserved.

No part of this book may be used or reproduced by any means, graphic, electronic, or mechanical, including photocopying, recording, taping, or by any information storage retrieval system without the written permission of the publisher except in the case of brief quotations embodied in critical articles and reviews.

ISBN 979-8-218-10231-9

To order books email:
gboylan@aol.com

Eli Clark and Gerry Boylan

Thanks to the Detroit Writing Room for their help with Firefly Island. We heartily recommend their services for writers.
www.detroitwritingroom.com

My first book is dedicated to my Mom and Dad.
Love, Eli.

Firefly Island is dedicated to Sue (Boylan) Charette,
my big sister and founder of the original Ghost Club.
Love, Gerry

Table of Contents

One: The Story Begins 7

Two: The Specials 12

Three: The One and Only Bernie Scala 22

Four: Slumgullion Stew 28

Five: Let's Get This Party Started! 36

Six: Fast Freddie Hatches His Plan 38

Seven: All Heck Breaks Loose 42

Eight: Through the Storm, A Ray of Light 45

Nine: The Plot Thickens 47

Ten: Everybody Get Ready! 52

Eleven: The Showdown 55

Twelve: The Battle Begins 59

Thirteen: Nuts! 68

Fourteen: Bernie to the Rescue 73

Fifteen: All Bad Things Must Come to an End 77

Denouement 85

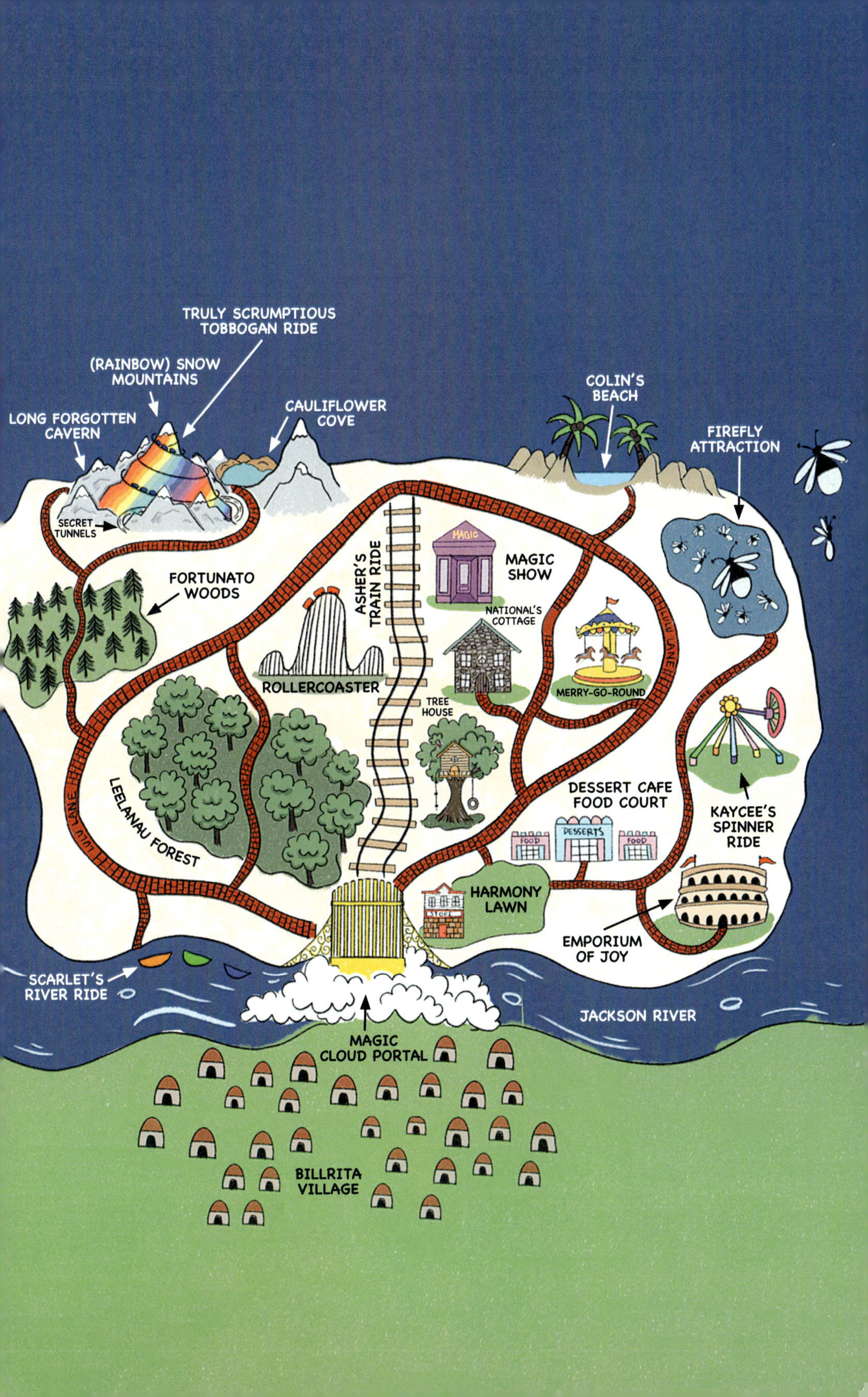
TRULY SCRUMPTIOUS TOBBOGAN RIDE
(RAINBOW) SNOW MOUNTAINS
LONG FORGOTTEN CAVERN
CAULIFLOWER COVE
COLIN'S BEACH
FIREFLY ATTRACTION
SECRET TUNNELS
FORTUNATO WOODS
ASHER'S TRAIN RIDE
MAGIC
MAGIC SHOW
NATIONAL'S COTTAGE
ROLLERCOASTER
MERRY-GO-ROUND
TREE HOUSE
LEELANAU FOREST
DESSERT CAFE FOOD COURT
FOOD
DESSERTS
FOOD
KAYCEE'S SPINNER RIDE
HARMONY LAWN
EMPORIUM OF JOY
SCARLET'S RIVER RIDE
JACKSON RIVER
MAGIC CLOUD PORTAL
BILLRITA VILLAGE

Chapter 1: The Story Begins

Not so long ago, in a place where dreams hung like apples ready to be picked, a fantastic place of merriment and delight was waiting for the signal to open its golden gates.

The quaint Village of Billrita overlooked the navy blue waters of the Jackson River. If you looked across the river, you would see a picturesque island sitting pretty as a postcard. Red brick paths ran through forests that met a towering mountain. The mountaintop was covered in snow with sweeping streaks of rainbow colors streaming down the middle. All of this was framed by a robin's-egg blue sky filled with fluffy ivory clouds moving across the sky from west to east. In front of this marvelous landscape, above two golden gates, hung a sign of shining letters. It proclaimed:

WELCOME TO THE FIREFLY ISLAND PARK OF WONDERS
ALL THE FUN UNDER THE SUN!

Children from all over the countryside did extra chores at home, went to bed without a moan or groan and were on their super-special-triple-dipple best behavior so their parents would take them to the park. They knew that Firefly Island Park promised them a day of all the fun under the sun, just like the sign said.

The owners of the park were Francis Fortunato and Dakota Leelanau. On this day, they were sitting contentedly in their rocking chairs on the front porch of their treehouse home. The treehouse was perched in a towering 100-year-old oak tree. From their roost overlooking the park, they viewed a kaleidoscope of sunrise colors that painted the sky. They had built their Park of Wonders 50 years ago when they were newlyweds and had owned and managed it with love ever since. Now, they were so old Dakota's knees whistled when she walked, and Francis's back chirped when he bent down. Firefly Island had been part of Dakota's family since her great-great-grandfather Chief Leelanau and great-great-grandma Nokomis first settled there.

Dakota *Francis*

Dakota was the last of Chief Leelanau's descendants and tribe. She and Francis didn't have children, so they built a park that would delight thousands and thousands of kids every summer. They loved their life together and seeing children's smiles and hearing their laughter brought joy to their hearts. But they were getting too old to oversee the park and looked forward to a quiet retirement in their quaint treehouse home. They had a plan to make it happen that started with finding their successors.

Many years earlier, Francis and Dakota had hired Nathan National, an eager young man who first started working for them as a handyman. He was a hard worker, could fix anything and was as smart as they come. He got promoted many times until finally, he was made the Chief Amusement Man, in charge of the whole park. Nathan, orphaned as a young boy, became the child Francis and Dakota never had, a member of their family. They mentored him and began to see him as their likely successor to manage the park.

Along the way, Nathan met a brilliant young lady, Aaliya, who was working a summer job in ticket sales at the park's Emporium of Joy attraction to help pay for her college tuition. They began to hang out together and found they enjoyed each other's company more and more. After work, they would stroll the park together, talking as they walked, late into the night. As these things sometimes go, they fell in love, became inseparable and started planning a future together.

Not long after Aaliya graduated and Nathan received a promotion, they were married under the big oak tree holding Francis and Dakota's tree house. The newly married couple loved the park and were thrilled when Aaliya was offered a full-time job as Dakota's assistant, helping to manage the park's finances. Even better, they were offered a place to live in an old cottage not far from their mentor's treehouse.

Soon enough, their family grew by two children, Eileen and Joe. They adopted a dog and named him Cookie and added a second story to their cottage for their growing family. It was a home filled with lots of games, laughter and love. Every day, the family woke up with a tickle in their toes and smiles as big as the Grand Canyon because they loved living and working at the amusement park.

Dakota and Francis felt blessed to be part of Nathan and Aaliya's family, with a double blessing that they were precisely the right people to take over the management of their park. They would retire this year on the 50th Anniversary of the park, and turn over control to Aaliya and Nathan. They would sell them the business, with payments made over the next 10 years, while continuing to live in their lovely treehouse home. It was a great deal all around.

Together they planned a big 50th Anniversary celebration and retirement party on the upcoming Opening Day of the park. They advertised a special promotion with a lottery and the 1,000 lucky winners were given a free pass to park for the big day. Everything was included, from the rides, attractions and all the famous treats and desserts you could eat. Everyone was looking forward to the celebration, which was tomorrow!

From their front porch, Francis and Dakota watched the National family and their fellow workers scurrying to put the final touches on the big party. Eleven-year-old Joe National was polishing the brass rails on the World's Biggest Merry-Go-Round. Nine-year-old Eileen National swept the walkway to the park clean as a whistle.

The National family was thrilled about the big celebration, but even more so about becoming the managers and owners.

"Tomorrow's the big day for us, Aaliya. Who can believe we're about to take over the Park of Wonders? That's a wonder in itself!" Nathan exclaimed.

"We've worked hard for this Nathan, but not for a minute do I forget how fortunate we have been to be taken under the wing of Dakota and Francis. We've been blessed. Let's agree to keep paying the blessing forward." Aaliya gave Nathan a big hug.

"Deal," agreed Nathan.

Chapter One: The Story Begins

It was a grand life for the National family. If the Lord was willing and the creek didn't rise, the family would soon be the owners of Firefly Island Park of Wonders. It would be a dream come true.

But there was something a-brewing, ever so slowly on Firefly Island. No one noticed a tiny grey cloud on the far horizon. It didn't look like much. These things rarely do. But it was getting darker and percolating like an old-fashioned coffee pot.
Maybe it was nothing. Or maybe it was.

Chapter Two: The Specials

The day before the 50th Anniversary celebration began the same as usual for Joe and Eileen, except for the extra chores in preparation for the big day.

Every summer morning, after their chores were complete, Eileen and Joe liked to take their own personal tour of the park. Today, Joe laced up his rollerblades and skated next to his sister, Eileen, riding her trusty bike, Bloopy. They were followed by Cookie, who laughed while he ran. That's right; he was a laughing dog. Instead of barking, Cookie would guffaw up a storm, although it sounded more like a cross between a chortle and snicker. When you heard it, you couldn't help but crack a smile and laugh yourself. Eileen and Joe loved Cookie, their lovable, laughing dog, who was as smart as they come. Eileen, who loved to take bike rides, would ride through the park with Cookie running alongside her bike. Joe, who loved to draw, would sit under the big oak tree with pencils and pad, with Cookie's head in his lap.

Chapter Two: The Specials

This morning Eileen biked, Joe roller-bladed and Cookie galloped down the path next to Asher's Train Ride. The path weaved through the middle of the park through a forest, around hills and through a lush vale, which is like a valley, but smaller. They were headed towards their favorite part of the park, where the Specials lived and worked.

The Specials were folks with unusual talents. While they couldn't leap tall buildings in a single bound, shoot flame balls, or anything super-duper like that, they brought miles of smiles and a belly full of laughs to everyone who visited their attractions. For as long as anyone could remember, the Specials were part of the legend and magic of the place. All of the rides were fantastically fun, but everyone agreed that the Special's attractions were astounding.

Eileen and Joe leaned into a downhill curve and picked up speed to start the uphill climb to Snow Mountain, near the far side of the island. This was the home of Kate and Stanley Snow, the first Special attraction on their park tour. The story goes that Kate and Mrs. Santa Claus were cousins. She certainly looked a lot like Mrs. Claus. The Snows had invented the Truly Scrumptious Toboggan Ride. It was on a glorious mountain that, instead of being covered with white snow, had all the colors of a rainbow and even better, tasted truly scrumptious. It was the world's largest snow cone!

A moving sidewalk like you see in airports would bring the ride's visitors up the mountain to the launching pad. Kate Snow welcomed visitors where the sidewalk began, encouraging visitors to have a fun and safe ride and to be careful to be polite to other riders. Her husband, Stanley Snow, waited at the top of the ride and led the children to their toboggan, giving each rider a spoon and paper cup. When everyone had their sled seat belts clicked on, Stanley would holler, "Let's go!" release the sled and "whoosh," off they'd go slaloming down the hill.

Eileen   *Joe*

On their way down the hill, the toboggan riders reached down with their spoons and scooped super delicious snow ice into their paper cups, laughing and slurping all the way down the flavored slope.

After they finished their ride down the hill, the children left with rainbow mustaches and ear-to-ear grins. Kate stood at the bottom of the hill with a smile that warmed the coldest heart. She handed her departing guests a tutti-frutti popsicle in case anyone wasn't full.

On this particular morning, Joe, Eileen and Cookie were greeted warmly by Kate. "By gosh, by golly, it's my favorite kids and dog in the whole world. Come for a ride did you, young lad and lassie? And Cookie, of course. Right this way."

Chapter Two: The Specials

Kate pointed them upward and they hustled up the hill. At the top, Stanley Snow gave each of them a big hug, along with a spoon and toboggan.

"Joe and Eileen, as I live and breathe, great to see you! Here's an extra-large spoon for your ride down the hill. We're testing them out to use for the big party tomorrow! And Cookie, you giggling canine, how are you this fine morning?" Stanley gave Cookie a big hug and tickled his belly, which started a festival of laughs between Cookie, the kids and Stanley.

"Now off with you, children!" and Stanley gave their toboggan a push-off, and down they slid, laughing and scooping snow-ice all the way. At the bottom, the kids hugged Kate and waved a thank you to Stanley. Off they went, slurping the last of their snow cone in one hand and a tutti-frutti popsicle in the other.

Eileen jumped back on her bike with her brother following on his rollerblades toward the next Special Attraction. They headed past their cottage toward Harmony Lawn and The Singing Swinging Dancing Prancing Emporium of Joy. Once there, they were met by Gentle Giant, known to children as GG. He was one of the most lovable men you'll ever meet, although he could be quite shy, often stuttering when he talked. All that changed when he was on stage and he transformed into an entertainer.

His partner in the Emporium was Robot Guy, who was very outgoing, the opposite of his pal. He had been a famous dancer in many Broadway shows until he decided to settle down. Together Robot Guy (also known as RG) and Gentle Giant formed a song and dance team that made the visitors want to join in the fun!

Eileen and Joe liked to stop by before the Emporium opened and take a quick spin on the dance floor and sing a song with GG and RG, which is what they did today.

"Look who's here to twirl on our dance floor!" Robot Guy said as he skimmed across the floor.

"Hey there, my little National friends, and of course, Cookie," boomed Gentle Giant.

"Top of the morning to you, Mr. Robot Guy and Mr. Giant," Eileen called out.

"Gentlemen, let's have a song and dance. What song do you suggest?" Joe bowed like a performer.

"Let's see, what will it be, my friend, Mr. Giant? How about Singing in the Rain or Dancing in the Street?"

"Oh, definitely Dancing in the Street! Motown is a great way to start our young friends' day!" Gentle Giant replied.

"Alright, let me start the music." RG selected the tune from the world's biggest jukebox, an old-fashioned music box featuring flashing lights and real records that flipped onto a turntable, ready to be played.

Eileen joined hands with Robot Guy and they twirled beautifully together. She was learning to be quite the dancer. GG leaned down and picked up Joe, sat him on his shoulders and joined in.

In addition to being a gifted vocalist, GG had a laugh that began in his colossal belly and rolled out of his mouth like an ocean wave. But what made him truly special was his melodious singing voice. It was the voice of an angel – a very large angel. Come to think of it; he sounded more like a choir of angels. When you heard him sing, it seemed impossible that so many magnificent sounds could fly out of his mouth. You almost felt like you were walking on the musical notes he crooned.

When GG sang, Robot Guy would dance and oh, how he could dance. He floated to his pal's songs, moving effortlessly from tap dancing to hip-hop, ballet, swing and Irish step dancing. When their performances started every day, doors would open and hundreds of children, parents and friends would rush in to fill the Robot Guy's dance floor. RG would find the person who was usually too bashful to dance and pull them up on stage and before you knew it, he or she was twirling gracefully.

This made everyone else feel comfortable dancing too. No matter how clumsy you might be, once you stepped onto Robot Guy's dance floor, you couldn't help boogieing like there was no tomorrow. Folks were doing the foxtrot, the samba, the mambo, disco duck, the running man, you name it, they were dancing it.

The happy-go-lucky dancing guests would shake, shimmy and roll until their hearts were full.

After the dancers had hoofed up a storm, Robot Guy introduced his world-renowned Robot Dance. The music and dance started in slow-motion, then he danced fast, faster and fastest until he became a blur. It was quite a sight to see hundreds of dancers join in, mimicking Robot Guy's high-speed dance moves. The big finish left everyone with just enough breath to cheer and shout! It was often said that the worst lousy mood could not survive at the Emporium of Joy.

Joe and Eileen were grateful for their special daily morning dance. It was a great way to start a day. They bid farewell to RG and Gentle Giant and returned home for lunch and some playtime with Cookie. The rest of their day depended on any extra chores or help needed around the park. They didn't mind helping out, but they were kids after all and what they liked to do most of all was play. The park was their playground and as long as they returned home after the street lights turned on, they were free to explore the park on their own, especially during summer vacation, which it was now.

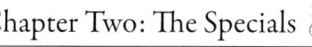

After dinner, with the sun fading like a giant orange gumdrop disappearing under the clouds, they asked their parents if they could visit the unique Special attraction call the Fantabulous Flight of the Fireflies. They knew not to ask too often, as it meant a late bedtime. With their parent's permission to make a quick visit before returning home for a bath, books and bed, Eileen and Joe biked and rollerbladed as fast as they could to the attraction. Cookie was close behind, laughing all the way,

The attraction was also a favorite place to end the day for the park's visitors. After a day of fun and play, the visitors were tired, with Cheshire cat grins on their faces. As the light of day melted into the delicious dark of night, they would stroll down the Purple Pathway that led to the firefly attraction. It was like nothing else you would find in this world. Firefly Island was named for these highly unusual fireflies.

"Hi Felipe. Hello Frida!" Joe and Eileen called out as they arrived. Felipe was a firefly, but not just any firefly. He was the son of the Empress of Fireflies (which is another story). Because he ate his fruit and veggies every day, exercised regularly and read a lot of books, he grew into a very large and unusually bright firefly. He was the size of a barn owl and his glow could be seen across Lake Michigan. His sister, Frida, was the most glowing firefly in the world, meaning she outshone all the other fireflies and smart as a cockatoo. Together, Frida and Felipe led the multitude of fireflies that lived on the island.

Did you know that fireflies are beetles but with built-in lanterns? Anyone who has seen the flickering lights of these talented insects as the sun sets and darkness begins knows it's a treat to see. The females light up to let the males know that they are interested in some romance, like a summertime date. It's really quite sweet, but a few females can get a little carried away and have been known to bite the leg off a male! But fear not, at Firefly Island, these unique fireflies are all peaceful. And while most fireflies only live one glorious year, these lightning bugs are special with much longer lives.

At the Fantabulous Flight Attraction, guests would recline in hammocks woven out of silk. As they lay relaxing, a blinking posse of fireflies appeared—a million of them. No kidding, a million fireflies! They would hover over the guests with their beacons of firefly light blinking, so it looked like the Milky Way was visiting earth. The fireflies then descended on the guests, covering them with dazzling light and gently lifting their hammocks into the sunset-lit sky. As the tiny wings of thousands of fireflies beat rhythmically fast, nature's lanterns twinkled hypnotically, mesmerizing the guests as they floated in the hammocks just long enough to feel peace before settling back down to earth.

And that is how a typically wonderful day at Firefly Island would end. Children would be droopingly weary, the kind of tired where they wished for a little more time to enjoy the day but couldn't keep their eyes open. Their heads found their way onto the shoulders of dads and moms as they headed for the park's exit, bringing calming dreams and sleeping smiles. It would be much the same for Eileen and Joe as their parents would tuck their tuckered-out children into bed. Their sleeping smiles seemed to be thanking their lucky stars for the blessings life had given them.

As night descended on Firefly Island and the moon rose in the east, the unnoticed little black cloud that had emerged in the corner of the park began to thunder. The shadows grew until it covered the moon and a storm's rumble shook the ground for miles. Bolts of lightning cracked overhead and everyone sleeping awoke with a fright. A strange sound filled the air. It was Cookie and he wasn't laughing. He was barking out a woeful howl. Sleep was not easy at Firefly Island that night.

No, something wasn't right on Firefly island. Not right at all.

Chapter Three:
The One and Only Bernie Scala

There was one more feature of the Firefly Island Amusement park that made it unique. It was called the Magic Cloud Portal and it was the gateway to the park. Bernadette (Bernie) Scala was a 12-year-old science prodigy who invented it using her knowledge of the time-space continuum. That's a mouthful and there's no easy way to explain it, but let's give it a shot.

The space-time continuum is all about dimensions. For example, a line drawn on paper has one dimension (1D), a square has two dimensions (2D), and a cube has three dimensions (3D). But there's a fourth dimension: time. When you add them all together, you get the space-time continuum. It's more complicated than that and you may not be interested in a science lesson, but this stuff is incredible. And that's what this portal is all about.

Up until a year ago, visitors to the park traipsed over a bridge from the mainland of the Village of Billrita to the shore of Firefly Island, a short walk to the park's entrance. That was until in the wee hours of an icy November morning, a massive windstorm huffed and puffed and blew the bridge down. It was a calamity, as the bridge was built 50 years earlier and took a year to complete. Without the bridge, there were no customers for the park.

That's where Bernie came into the picture. Bernadette, who preferred her nickname, Bernie, lived in the village with her granny Gertie, who was as old as the hills. She was her only family. After the bridge blew down, she stood on the Village shore with her grandma and watched Francis and Dakota row ashore in a park rowboat.

"What are we going to do, Francis?" Dakota asked. "It will take months and months to rebuild the bridge. We could go broke if we didn't open for customers. There aren't enough boats to ferry our visitors."

Francis was stumped. It didn't look good.

Just then, Gertie piped up in her squeaky voice. "Talk to my granddaughter, Bernie. She's an inventor, don'tcha know. Bernie's been transporting goats in our backyard through a cloud. Quite a sight it is, watching goats travel through a space-time continuum cloud!"

Francis and Dakota looked quizzically at Gertie, who they had known for a long time. They weren't sure where she was going with this story, but they knew while she could be odd, she was also highly intelligent. Gertie was a scientist when she was young and had taught her super-intelligent granddaughter Bernie everything she knew. Bernie was a shy kid and listening to her Grandma's compliments, she blushed a bright red.

Dakota, who could make a radish smile, walked over to Bernie and said, "Young lady, I have a feeling you're special. Can you show us your goats and clouds?"

That's how it began.

Even at Bernie's young age, she had studied Albert Einstein's theories and had come up with her invention. She created a cloud that could transport an object a short distance to another point. She started out small, transporting LEGO blocks, then carrots and prunes. Her first

Chapter Three: The One and Only Bernie Scala

experiments on living things were with ants and spiders, who showed up on the other side of the portal just fine, although they did run in small circles for a minute. Bernie's test moved to larger animals like gerbils, voles (like moles, but vegetarians), an adventurous raccoon family, and a small herd of goats.

She noticed that the goats seemed worried entering the portal, bleating out their concern. But, when they exited the other side, they were singing a different tune, literally. Their "maaaah's" were musical. When Bernie sent one group of goats through, the group came out bleating out a goat version of Seventy Six Trombones from The Music Man, the musical. They were smiling up a storm, too. Whatever was happening for those few short seconds in the cloud was good! After the goats, Bernie and her grannie Gertie decided to give it a whirl themselves. It worked fine and the two came out singing showtunes and dancing the polka.

Francis and Dakota walked over to Gertie's garage, which was also Bernie's laboratory. After watching a demonstration with the goats, they were amazed and knew it could be a terrific replacement for the bridge. It took a lot of further testing to prove that the cloud portal was safe not only for goats but also for people. Finally, all the approvals were complete. Dakota and Francis tested it themselves to make sure all systems were "go" and the portal was ready for their guests.
Bernie had designed the portal to look like a giant caterpillar, but depending on the weather, it would change shape. She dubbed it the Magic Cloud Portal. The park's guests would enter on a deck on the shore of the Village and poof; a few seconds later, they'd arrive onto Firefly Island and voila, they would be at the park's entrance gates! The guest were wowed by the experience, some describing the short trip like flying in a dream. Other guests noted that they entered the portal in a terrible mood but exited smiling up a storm. It was an instant success!

Bernie was a hero. The portal was so popular that attendance at the park soared. Francis and Dakota built Bernie and her grannie a gumdrop house next door to the gates of the park. They also gave her a royalty payment for each visitor that used the portal and a part-time job as the Chief Technology Wizard. Most importantly, they introduced her to the National family, who welcomed Bernie with open arms. Because of her shyness, Bernie didn't have many friends in the Village of Billrita. And other than Joe and Eileen, and now Bernie, no other children lived on the island. Sure, there were plenty of kids visiting the park, but that wasn't the same as having friends. Adding to that, Joe and Eileen were home-schooled by their mom. Bernie joined their classes and it added some spice to classes.

Bernie was a math and science genius and Eileen loved both subjects, so they worked on experiments together and had a blast. Joe was more of a reading and writing kind of boy, which wasn't his sister or Bernie's strong suit, so he tutored them and taught them how to play stories in the round. He'd start a story and then hand it off to their new pal who made up her part, passed it to Eileen and before you knew it, they were coming up with a ridiculous tale with made up characters and wild battles. All out of their imaginations!

One of the experiments all three of the kids worked on together started with Bernie's observations that the weather on Firefly Island was truly unusual. It seemed to be affected by the people's emotions on the island. She detected that the weather always seemed sunny and mild when the park was in full swing and laughter and good times filled the air. But, if there happened to be a bunch of visitors who were cranky and in bad moods, which did happen every now and again, the sky would cloud up. Even though the park was a place of fun and joy, it was still real life and let's face it, people still get angry, disobedient, scared, scrape a knee, and get into a fight with a brother or sister. I'm sure you understand.

Bernie noticed this and along with Joe and Eileen, they began recording the mood of the park by observing the park's visitors and then checking it against the weather. They recorded their data into a spreadsheet. Bernie thought that if emotions could control the weather, they would be onto something big! On the evening before the big retirement party, after all the guests had left the island, there was a burst of thunder that startled the trio. They all looked up at the sky and the darkening clouds looked like they were having a wrestling match. It was odd. What was causing it, they wondered? They were going to find out soon enough.

Chapter Four: Slumgullion Stew

While the storm raged, off in the farthest corner of the island, a motley group of no-goodniks was approaching in a boat. The boat was pulled by a massive narwhal, who wasn't bothered by the roaring winds and topsy-turvy waves.

The narwhal's name was Nervous Norvus and he was paid a handsome price to transport the stinkiest, slimiest band of baddies ever known to this part of the world. They were called the Slumgullion Squad and their leader was Fast Freddie Fortunato. He was the twin brother of Francis Fortunato. Freddie and Francis had been the best friends growing up, as identical twin brothers tend to be. But that had ended long ago.

Growing up, they both loved sports, books and amusement parks and they did everything together. They were both outstanding baseball players, with Freddie being just a little bit better than his brother. Francis was a second baseman, Freddie, a shortstop and they were experts at the double play. Both dreamed of winning baseball scholarships so that they could afford college.

They read the same books, mostly biographies of sports stars, but they liked books about any historical heroes. They also loved amusement parks and vowed they would open their own park together when they grew up. Freddie had drawn up pictures of his version of a Wild Mouse ride, which was a kind of rollercoaster, but with tighter turns and not as tall. He was sure it would be a big hit.

It was a great childhood and Freddie and Francis were as close as two twin brothers could be. Then, just before they graduated from high school, it all fell apart.

Chapter Four: Slumgullion Stew

It started as a baseball game accident. In the late innings of their high school championship game, a high hopper whistled past their pitcher's ear and was headed right over second base. It was a toss-up who should field it; Francis at second or Freddie at shortstop. They both raced to the ball at the same time. At the last second, it looked like it would be Freddie's ball, so Francis tried to turn away. Too late! Just as the ball hit Freddie's mitt, his foot stepped on top of Francis' shoe – and twisted.

Freddie screamed in pain, but he still made the throw to first – out! He collapsed on the field and had to be helped off the field by his brother. Freddie's ankle was shattered.

Apr 13 1972

In the bottom of the ninth, with the bases loaded, Francis hit a long single down the first base line (he was a lefty hitter), knocking in two runs that gave their team a walk-off championship. While an injured Freddie looked on, his brother Francis was hoisted on his teammate's shoulders. At first, Freddie was happy for his brother.

Later, Freddie found out how badly he was injured. He needed pins in his ankle and by the time he recovered, he knew his dream of college scholarship was gone. When his twin Francis received a full scholarship, his thoughts started to twist and turn. He was jealous.

Freddie was glum. Then bummed. Then grumpy and finally bitter as vinegar. He started to think that his brother had stepped under his foot on purpose so that he could be the hero. Freddie took it a step further, imagining Francis had a diabolical plan to injure him and get him out the way. He couldn't get the idea out of his head and there it grew into a big, rolling ball of resentment for his brother, who he had always loved. That's the thing about envy: when it gets ahold of you, it grows as fast as blue mold on old bread.

After high school graduation, their friendship took a turn for the worse. Francis found a job as a lifeguard at their town pool. Because of his ankle injury, Freddie was stuck at home, where he passed the time reading books about famous criminals who had made fortunes. Francis tried to talk to his brother after work about their plans for the future, but Freddie started arguing with his brother. Just before summer ended, an argument turned into a wrestling match which ended up with the slightly stronger Freddie on top of his brother, fist raised.

"I hate you, Francis. You caused my ankle to break and stole all the glory. I–I could just slug you!"

"Go ahead, Freddie, if it makes you feel better. But you know I didn't hurt you."

Francis came within an inch of punching his brother in the nose but then jumped off him.

"I don't ever want to talk to you again, Francis! I'm going to be famous someday and you'll just be a washed-up ballplayer without me. You'll see!"

Freddie stormed away from his brother.

That was it. They didn't speak to each other for a very, very long time. Soon after their fight, Freddie and Francis went their separate ways. Francis went off to college alone, played baseball and studied engineering and architecture. He met Dakota at college, where she was studying Construction Management. They fell in love and moved to Firefly Island, where Dakota had grown up. Together, they built the Firefly Island Park of Wonder. The dream he had shared with his brother Freddie had come true. But not for Freddie.

Freddie's life took him in the opposite direction as he left home and drifted across the country by himself. Before long, he was a velcro vest of bad habits that stuck to him and wouldn't let go. He drifted and grifted, making money with schemes to cheat people. He was very good at his new craft, earning the nickname Fast Freddie. Over time, he organized a gang and they were so clever, the police never caught them. They traveled the world, hatching plans to make more and more money. Although he was definitely a crook, he made a point to only steal from the very wealthy. Once he found out his scam had cost a poor grandmother her life savings, he sent her the money back with a note apologizing. So, there was some good left in Freddie, but not much.

Freddie was living in Madagascar planning his next crime when he happened to read a magazine article about Francis Fortunato and the Firefly Island Park of Wonders' 50th-anniversary celebration. His blood began to boil as he glared at a picture of his twin brother with his wife Dakota in front of the Magic Cloud Portal. As he read about the big party for their retirement party, steam started puffing out his ears. He had tried for all these years to forget his brother, and here he was staring at his picture in the newspaper with his lovely wife. He looked so happy.

His brother Francis had lived their dreams without him! Oh, this made him madder than an angry bull. All of the lousy feelings toward his brother came rushing back like wet fish smacking cold lips. He Googled his brother, the park, his wife Dakota, Firefly Island and the magic cloud portal. The more he learned, the more he stewed. It didn't take long to concoct a dastardly plan to ruin his brother's big day and all he had built, even if it meant traveling halfway across the world to do it!

Fast Freddie assembled his gang, the Slumgullion Squad. If you've never had slumgullion stew, it's a clean-out-the-refrigerator kind of ghoulash, meaning anything just about to go bad goes into the brew. That pretty much describes the Slumgullion Squad, a cast of misfits, a potent group of troublemakers, cheats and thieves.

The Squad had been assembled over several years, handpicked by Freddie for their various skills of mayhem. They had all been with Freddie for years, except for one recent addition.

Tootie O'Fartster's name pretty much summed him up. If he walked into a room, it started to smell really, really bad. And his personality was as rank as the aura of his odor. He could make anyplace stink! He was the Sultan of Smelly. Tootie could clear out a room faster than a skunk, which came in handy in many crimes. He specialized in cooking up awful smells, but he also concocted special potions that could put people to sleep and even hypnotize them.

Snake Lady was a snake charmer and she had a bag of snakes that looked and sounded so scary; they scared each other! They were harmless snakes, but no one knew that and if you needed to frighten someone in a scam, Snake Lady and her snakes could scare the bejabbers out of anyone.

Chapter Four: Slumgullion Stew

33

Nervous Norvus, the narwhal, was the muscle of the gang. Narwhals are the sea's unicorns and usually live out of the way in places where very few people see them. They are technically whales but cousins to porpoises. Norvus was unusually large for a narwhal and his pointy tusk was quite a sight, not to mention a weapon. He received his nickname from his narwhal tribe because whenever he had misbehaved, which he did a lot, his whiskers twitched nervously. Norvus had been banished from his tribe for stealing other narwhals' fish. Soon after, he met Fast Freddie and joined the squad. He was used in capers that involved water and needed extra-strong muscles.

Fast Freddie

Tootie O'Fartser

snake Lady

curly chameleon

Nervous Narwhal

Chameleon Curly, the youngest member of the squad, had just recently joined. He could blend into the scenery anywhere, picking pockets faster than a herd of speeding grasshoppers. Freddie had met him when Curly had pickpocketed his watch. He didn't get far as Freddie had a network of spies, one of whom reported where Curly and his watch could be found. He admired Curly's skill and hired him – after his watch was returned, of course.

The gang assembled quickly for this new job, chartering a hot air balloon with a jet engine to fly them over the ocean for a landing close to the backside of Firefly Island. Instead of the usual hot air balloon basket, the passengers were carried in a deep jolly-boat, an old-fashioned vessel used as a ferry between ships. It was big enough to hold the gang, about twenty feet long and easy to row or sail, depending on what was needed. They landed at night, and the jolly-boat now doubled as their transport to the island, since landing the balloon on the island might attract attention. The balloon was released and Norvus slipped over the side and into a harness attached to the front of the boat and started to swim.

Norvus's powerful swimming propelled the gang toward their destination, Cauliflower Cove. It was located on Firefly Island's remote far side, nestling up to Snow Mountain. At the back of the cove was a hidden cave called the Long Forgotten Cavern that burrowed into Snow Mountain. Landing on the large, flat boulders outside the cave, the Squad shook off the rain from the storm and waves and waited for their instructions from their fearsome leader, Fast Freddie.

"Fellow slumgullions, our work here begins tomorrow morning, on the day that my brother celebrates 50 years of success. Success he stole from me! Our job is to ruin the celebration, chase off the customers, kidnap my brother and his lovely wife and force him to turn all the park over to me. Finally, I will have an amusement park of my own, more money, fame and everything that is rightfully mine. And you'll all have a share of it if you do your worst to my brother!"

Freddie's eyeballs were rolling around in his head like pinballs. He was going nutsy cuckoo! The gang loved it and cheered him and the plan.

"OK. Everyone inside this cave and get some shut-eye. We start our Plan of Doom and Gloom tomorrow morning at the crack of dawn," Freddie concluded.

The weather had worsened, especially at the Cove, as a heap of woe and worry had arrived at Firefly Island and was about be unleashed. Unless something or someone could stop it.

Chapter Five:
Let's Get This Party Started

The big day of celebration dawned beautiful and sunny and the happiest place under the sun was abuzz with activity. The National family, the Specials, all the park's staff, Dakota and Francis had completed all the preparations for the 50th Anniversary party. All 1,000 of the guests who had won the lottery for free tickets were excitedly lining up in the Village of Billrita to enter the park. Bernie was warming up the Magic Cloud Portal and was minutes away from letting the crowd enter.

Everyone was in their places, with Dakota and Francis ready at the park's island entrance to greet their guests. It was a bittersweet day for them. Even though they weren't going anywhere, they were retiring after 50 years of doing what they loved. After today, the Nationals would be in charge, although their mentors would still live on the island and be available to provide help and advice.

Francis gave the Fantabulous Fortunato Marching Band a signal to begin their first song and dance routine to get the party started. The Specials heard the band and tooted their unique horns to signal they were ready, followed by all the other attractions and rides doing the same. The park clowns readied their balloons and honked their noses. Over on the shores of the Village, Bernie pressed the start button and the Magic Portal appeared and opened up. Families streamed through it. They were almost flying into the park with wings on their feet and a song in their hearts. It was time for the party to begin!

It wasn't long before every ride and attraction was going strong and laughter, whoops, hoots, hollers and shrieks of excitement filled the air. Francis and Dakota strolled through their beloved park arm-in-

Chapter Five: Let's Get This Party Started

arm. They watched as their protege Nathan made sure everything was running smoothly. Aaliya was directing a family to Snow Mountain, and Joe and Eileen were checking to see if the Delightful Desserts Cafe needed any supplies.

"It looks like everything is going very well, Francis," Dakota said.

"Yes, we're lucky to have found Nathan and Aaliya. Although, I am a little sad about not being in charge anymore." Francis's eyes were misty with tears.

"It will be fine, dear. It's time for us to step back and relax. It's not like we're going anywhere. We'll just be able to take longer naps and not get the emergency calls anymore."

"You're right, as always. I do like my naps!"

Francis and Dakota were thrilled that their big party was going to be a success. The National family was doing a great job. The beloved park was in good hands. They strolled back to their Tree House home for a long and contented nap. They did notice the dark clouds and thunder, which surprised them because it was nearly always sunny on the island. What they didn't know was that trouble was brewing along with storm clouds on the other side of the island.

Chapter Six:
Fast Freddie Hatches His Plan

In the Long Forgotten Cavern, Fast Freddie was awake early. Today he would finally get his revenge. He had read about the plans for his brother and his wife to retire and sell the park to his longtime managers, the Nationals. His goal was to use his squad to ruin the big party and, in all the confusion, kidnap Francis and Dakota and force them to sign the park over to him. He had gone over the plan in detail with his pals and they were all confident they could make it work.

The Slumgullion Squad woke up one-by-one until they all stood together, waiting for the signal from their boss to put their nefarious plans into action. Freddie stood in front of his gang and in a pirate voice, he pronounced, "Aaaarrgghh! My matey's of mayhem, the time has come. You have your instructions. Opening time for the park was an hour ago and I'm sure all the guests are having a blast. But, not for long! It's time to get to your positions and give my brother your worst. After you all unleash your first wave of woe, folks will be running around like squirrels chased by a pack of chihuahuas. Bad news travels fast and when their big celebration is a mess, guests will run for the exits. Then we'll spring part two of our plan! When we're successful and I own this park, the money will come rolling in and there will be enough for all of us to be rich, rich, rich!"

With that, Fast Freddie gathered his motley gang into a circle. "Hands in, mateys! One-two-three, HULLABALOO AND TROUBLE TOO!"

The Squad jumped into the jolly boat and Norvus swiftly pulled them to the rarely used Colin's Beach, located close to the Cove. This was their meeting place and when their dirty deeds were done, they would toot on their signal whistles and Norvus would return to pick them up.

Chapter Six: Fast Freddie Hatches His Plan

After Curly, Snake Lady and Tootie were dropped off on the beach, they split up and began their rotten work. Snake Lady glided away to a spot near the middle of the park and opened up her Bag O'Snakes. She gave instructions to 57 of the scariest-looking snakes you ever saw and they slithered off in 57 different directions.

Chameleon Curly was off in a flash, changing shapes and colors as he made his way near the park entrance. He started picking pockets so fast, he was a blur of burglary. Visitors were missing wallets, watches, coolers, hats, purses, sunglasses, and heck; Curly even snatched a toupee off an unsuspecting bald man!

Tootie O'Fartster moved quickly around trees and rocks until he was near Kate's Spinner Ride. Hiding in a grove of trees, he opened up his rolling suitcase and took out a kit labeled Stinkeroo Surprises. He set a big pot on a tree stump and started adding ingredients from various jars he pulled out of the suitcase.

Then he started chanting:

"I'm Tootie O'Fartster, so hold your nose,
What you're going to smell isn't a rose!
I'm Tootie O'Fartster, so run pell-mell,
Because here comes a batch of the Really Big Smell!"

As he sang, he stirred in a glob of skunkweed, a goop of penguin poop, a log of Limburger cheese, a dose of otter spraint and assorted other nose-holding odoriferous fixings that began to bubble and belch until a mist of a horrid fume rose and wafted like a ghoulish cloud that drifted toward the attractions and rides. It wasn't long before the park's guests started getting their first sniff of the nasty waft of bad air.

Today Nervous Norvus had two jobs. The first was to provide transportation for the gang back and forth between Cauliflower Cove and Colin's Beach. The second was to work with Fast Freddie to disrupt the Magic Cloud Portal. After dropping off the team and boat, Freddie jumped on Norvus's broad back and with powerful thrusts from his tail fin, Norvus propelled them to the other side of the island. They cruised low in the water until they spied the magic cloud portal. Today, it was green and shaped like a Spicebush Swallowtail Butterfly Caterpillar. As Freddie and Norvus approached, they took a big breath and slipped underwater. They emerged right in the middle of the portal. Norvus's tusk had speared through the marshmallow-like cloud floor, creating a seam they popped right through, some portal goop sticking to them as they did.

Being inside of the portal was like floating on a sponge. Freddie was smiling, truly happy for the first time in a month of Sundays. He took a box out of his cloak pocket and opened it, exposing a glowing tourmaline crystal. It pulsed like a beating heart. He had bought the crystal from an evil shaman while in Madagascar. (A shaman is like a minister for supernatural beings, like ghosts. Most shamans use their mystical powers for good, but like almost all professions, there are always bad apples). Freddie knew if he concentrated very hard, the crystal would interrupt the energy flow that made the Magic Portal work. Yes, Freddie was a bad guy, but he had done his research.

Chapter Six: Fast Freddie Hatches His Plan

Freddie stood up straight and held the crystal high over his head. The pulses of crystal colors changed from emerald green to pink, neon blue, copper, brilliant yellow and finally black. The glowing rays grew longer, reaching out until they touched the inside of the portal cloud.

Suddenly, the air started to shake. There was a blinding FLASH of light! A BOOM like thunder! Followed by a WHOOMPH. And then...

Well, you'll have to wait a minute to find out what happened next.

Chapter Seven:
All Heck Breaks Loose

Meanwhile, the Grand Retirement Party was picking up steam. All 1,000 of the guests were having a great time in the park. The boys and girls ran ahead of their parents to enjoy the attractions, rides and delicious treats. Shrieks of joy could be heard from the Scrumptious Toboggan Run and singing rang out from the Emporium of Joy. Felipe, Frida and the fireflies patiently waited for the crowd to enjoy the Mystical Merry-Go-Round, the Wildest Mouse Roller Coaster, the Abracadabra Magic Show, Kaycee's Spinner Ride, Asher's Train Ride, the Delightful Desserts Cafe and all the other fun stuff.

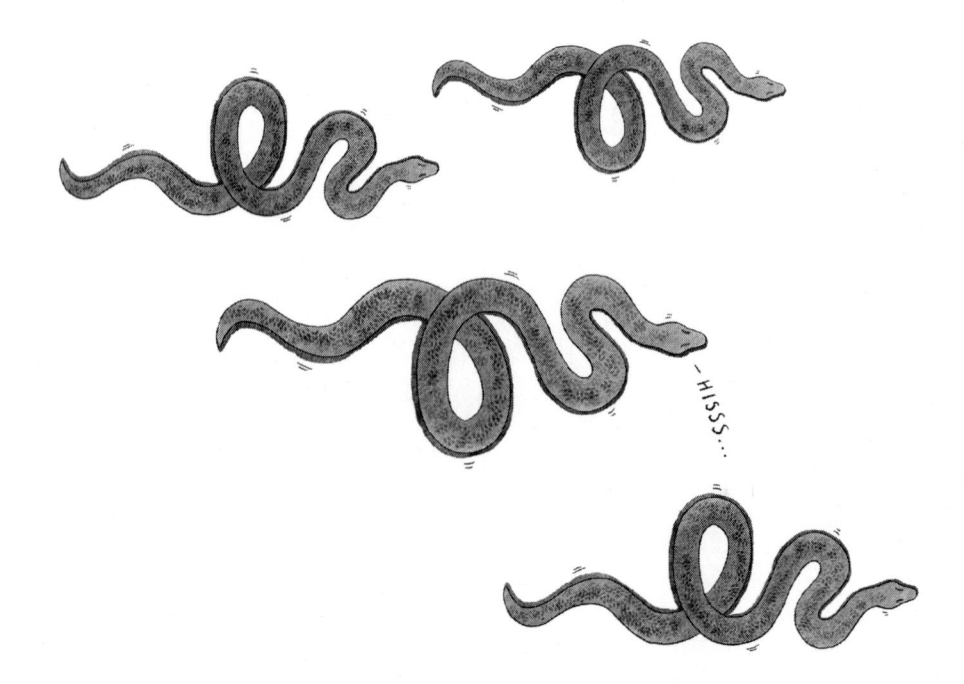

— HISSS...

Chapter Seven: All Heck Breaks Loose

While Frida, Felipe and their firefly friends waited for dusk, they enjoyed a sing-a-long led by Frida, who had a beautiful soprano voice. She had just finished the song Come Fly With Me and was leading all the fireflies into a rousing version of the Wind Beneath My Wings. Guests could hear the marvelous melodies waft across the park.

Suddenly, the air started to smell–I hate to say it–like farts! Something worse than fishy was wafting across the park. The fireflies started pointing at each other.

"It wasn't me!" said Fatima Firefly.

"Not me, either! replied Fitzroy Firefly.

"You smelt it. You dealt it!" Fanny Firefly hollered.

And on and on it went; there were a million fireflies after all!

The smell became worse and worse as it spread through the park. Tootie was cackling with twisted joy from his hiding spot.

"Holy Moly, something's rotten on Firefly Island!" a dad exclaimed. He held his nose as he waited for his kids to get off the Mystical Merry-Go-Round.

"Oy vey, someone let the gas out of the bag!" a park maintenance worker groaned.

Meanwhile, Snake Lady's snakes were slithering hither and yon. Even though her snakes were harmless, the guests didn't know that. Snakes waggled their reptile heads back and forth and let loose scary sounds like "HISSSS!" It scared the bejeebers out of the guests who panicked and jumped on picnic tables, scampered up nearby apple trees, or just ran fast as they could in the opposite direction, pushing strollers and picking up children along the way.

Freddie and Nervous Norvus were on the move, too. They were in the water looking back to where the Magic Portal Cloud used to be. Freddie's crystal had done its work. After the big boom, the cloud melted into the water like butter in a hot pan. Now, there was no way for guests to leave the island other than a few rowboats.

Norvus was pleased with the results and started making Narwhal noises like whistling, clicking and buzzing and a sound like a toy trumpet. It was his way of celebrating. He and his boss, Fast Freddie, had done their dirty deed. Freddie wore a crooked grin on his face. In the distance, they could hear sounds of chaos coming from the park. The plan must be working!

"Norvus, great job! But we're not done yet. Let's get back to the beach. It's time for Phase Two!"

Freddie hopped on the narwhal's back and Norvus slapped his tail fin on the water and powered away from shore. They passed by the entrance sign promising All the Fun Under the Sun.

"More like All the Bummers Under the Sun," Norvus snarked to no one in particular.

"All this will be mine soon! Mwahaha!" Freddie devilishly snorted.

Oh, it was a bleak day in the Park of Wonder. It just couldn't get any worse.

Could it?

Chapter Eight:
Through the Storm, A Ray of Light

The National family and Francis and Dakota were trying their best to calm their guests, but it was a lost cause. A thousand guests were headed toward the Magic Cloud Portal to go home, still unaware that the portal was long gone.

Bernie Scala knew what had happened. She had been in the Portal's maintenance shed near the park's entrance inspecting equipment when she heard the BOOOOOM and WHOOMPH. She opened the shed door and saw…nothing!

Bernie was thunderstruck as she stood looking at her finest invention now – gone! While she was a shy kid, she was also brave. She didn't panic, and instead of running away, she ran to the water's edge. There she saw an extraordinary sight; a giggling older man riding on the back of a narwhal. He was swimming fast around a bend, headed toward Colin's Beach, on the other side of the island.

Bernie thought this narwhal must be very far from home because they live in much colder water than the sea around Firefly Island. And the man on the whale's back looked strangely familiar, just like her boss and mentor, Francis! They were a very suspicious duo, especially as it looked like they were making a getaway from a crime scene.

She ran back to the shed, booted up her laptop, and started doing research. Bernie was an expert investigator and it wasn't long before she was looking at a Canadian Royal Mountie Wanted Poster for one Fast Freddie Fortunato! After a little more research, she unearthed a newspaper picture of two twin brothers playing high school baseball – Freddie and Francis!

She read on about a band of criminals called the Slumgullion Squad that Freddie led. A few more minutes and she had pictures of Nervous Norvus, Snake Lady, Chameleon Curly and Tootie O'Fartster and a list of crimes committed from Michigan to Timbuktu.

Now that Bernie knew the link between twin brothers Freddie and Francis Fortunato was at the heart of the disappearance of the portal, she picked up her laptop and made a beeline for Francis and Dakota's Treehouse. There was a mystery to be solved and Bernie Scala was just the girl to do it. As she ran toward the big oak tree, she began to see and smell some of the chaos in the park. The big day was going sour and she needed to help!

As Bernie streaked toward the treehouse, a fog descended and she could barely see anything in front of her. She slowed to a jog and thought: Hmmm, I've never seen fog on the island before. If my weather theory is correct, bad people doing bad things might be causing bad weather. That could be worth remembering.

Towards the middle of the island, thunder rumbled, followed by the CRAAACK of lightning. Bernie wondered what kind of bad things were happening there. She picked up her pace. Even in the heavy fog, she knew the way by heart.

"Think positive thoughts," she murmured to herself. "We'll get through this, whatever the heck it is!"

Chapter Nine:
The Plot Thickens

The National family and The Specials gathered in the shade of the giant oak and the Treehouse. In the midst of the chaos on the island they needed to figure out what the heck was going on and what to do about it. No one had seen Francis and Dakota for quite some time, which was strange because they would have been the first to try and make heads or tails of the situation in the Park.

Robot Guy was pacing back and forth, hands behind his back, biting his lip. Sally and Stanley Snow and Grandma Gertie sat in Adirondack chairs with worried looks on their faces. Gentle Giant's head reached the branches of the tree as his shuffling feet were digging trenches. It was hard to see through the leaves, but it looked like he had tears in his eyes. The National family, including Cookie, was sitting at a picnic table, the kid fidgeting, not knowing what to do. Nathan and Aaliya knew that with Dakota and Francis nowhere to be found, they needed to lead. Nathan took a deep breath and spoke first.

"This is my report," Nathan said somberly. "We have snakes running all over the island. One found its way onto the Ferris Wheel and scared the daylights out of the riders. No reported snake bites, just a lot of frightened folks. Then there are the smells. Horrible! Last of all, people are getting pickpocketed out of money, keys, watches. The thief even stole a pacifier from a baby. Every time one of our security folks thinks they see the perpetrator, the thief disappears into thin air."

Aaliya added, "I'm fairly sure that all of our guests are headed back to the portal to get off the island. Even our associates are holding their noses and asking if they can go home. It's a disaster and we need to find out who and why."

"I think I know why!" Bernie was huffing and puffing as she ran up to her friends. "But first, the bad news. The Magic Portal is gone and there are not enough rowboats to get people back to the Village of Billrita. That's the bad news. The good news is, I can fix it, but we may have bigger problems. Did you know that Mr. Fortunato has a twin brother? A criminal named Freddie, Fast Freddie."

The Nationals and the Specials were flabbergasted. This was news to them. When they heard about the Slumgullion Squad, they shook their heads. Bernie told them all about how Fast Freddie and his gang were behind all the trouble.

"Oh my goodness gracious, a twin brother? Who's a criminal? What next?" Sally Snow declared.

"Heavens to Murgatroyd," shouted Robot Guy. "That's a complete surprise. And this Freddie Fortunato is causing all the trouble?"
"It must be tough for Francis if he's kept this a secret from all of us," Aaliya said.

Everyone shook their head in agreement—what a shocking surprise.

Then Nathan's cell phone rang, bringing everyone to attention. On the other end was a raspy voice.

"Hello there, Mr. National. I'm your worst nightmare calling, Freddie Fortunato, the smarter twin brother of your boss, Francis. You're having some big troubles at my brother's park, aren't you? That's just a taste of what my gang and I can do. What you don't know is that sitting right next to me are your bosses. They are just fine and dandy, but they are my hostages!"

Chapter Nine: The Plot Thickens

It turned out that earlier in the day, Tootie had been secretly tracking Francis and Dakota. He had been hiding behind the big oak tree waiting for them to arrive. When they did, he opened his hand and blew a hypnosis potion toward them. The red and green dust swirled around their heads. They closed their eyes and when they opened them, both Francis and Dakota were in a trance.

Tootie whispered to them, "Come hither, come yon, come follow me. Follow me."

They did, right to Colin's Beach where Freddie and Nervous Norvus were waiting to whisk them away to their hideout in Cauliflower Cove. Francis, still in a trance, didn't recognize his brother. Freddie, who hadn't seen his brother in forever, almost forgot he hated his twin. That feeling only lasted a minute, though. In a flash, he had his hostages in the jolly boat, tied up and on their way to their hideout. A spray of the water woke up both Francis and Dakota. Although a little confused at first, when Francis saw his twin brother, Freddie, he couldn't believe it.

"Freddie? My brother? What in the name of all that's holy is going on?"

"That's a good question, brother," said Freddie as he flashed a wicked grin. "One you're going to get answered very soon!"

This reunion of long-lost twin brothers was not going well. At least not for Francis.

Nathan's face turned red with anger when he heard this news over the phone, but he kept his cool. "How do we get Francis and Dakota safe and back with us?" he replied.

"Good question, Nathan," said Freddie. "It's simple. You're going to work for me. You write up a contract that makes me your new boss. I know about your deal to buy my brother and Dakota out. Tear up your deal with my cheating brother. I'm going to be the new owner and as soon as we sign up our deal, my brother and his wife will be escorted out of the park forever. Otherwise, well, let's just say your favorite people will never be seen again! Bwahahaha!"

"Ok, Fred," Nathan replied and shifted his feet nervously "We'll do what you want. It will just take me some time to get the paperwork done."

"You have until sunset tonight, Nathan. I'll call you at dusk for the meet-up. And don't try any funny business. My gang and I aren't in the mood for games."

"Understood." Nathan turned off his phone and turned to the group.

Kate and Stanley Snow, Felipe and Frida, Robot Guy and Gentle Giant, Aaliya, Eileen and Joe, Bernie, Gertie and even Cookie, the laughing dog, listened to Nathan repeat the bad news. They were all stunned into silence.

"There are three ways you can act when the world turns upside down," Nathan told them. "You can panic and run away, become paralyzed with fear and do nothing, or you can rally your friends and family and do your best to make things right. Me, I'm going to fight back and find a way to rescue Francis and Dakota and our park!"

Everyone there felt the same way.

"Me too!" Joe pumped his fist in agreement with his dad.

"Let's fight!" Gertie jumped to her feet.

Chapter Nine: The Plot Thickens

"Right on, Nathan!" Gentle Giant bellowed.

"Yippetyyappetyyap!" Cookie laughed/barked loudly.

The group all joined in and there were high fives all around.

"I'm with you too," Bernie spoke up in her quiet voice. "I've been doing some research and I have some information I think we can use to make a plan to beat this gang."

Everyone turned to look at bespectacled Bernie. She had a map, a laptop and a plan. It was the first step in the right direction since the big day had turned to muck.

Through the storm clouds, a single ray of sunshine streamed down.

Maybe the tide was beginning to turn!

Chapter 10
Everybody Get Ready!

Bernie knelt and spread out a large map of Firefly Island and everyone huddled around her.

"Here's what we know so far. The cause of this mess is Fred Fortunato and he has a long-lasting vendetta against his twin brother – our boss – Francis. It dates back to their childhood and Fred, or Fast Freddie as he's known, has carried the grudge all these years. It's festered into what happened today: Blowing up the Magic Portal, sending his gang out to do dastardly deeds and worse of all, holding Francis and Dakota hostage. That's the status. Now the plan. Our to-do list includes:

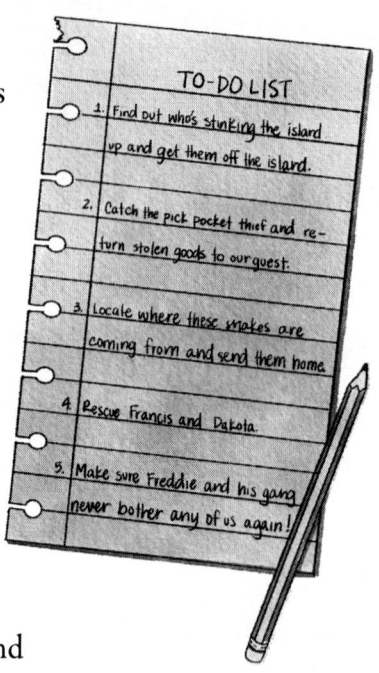

1. Find out who's stinking the island up and get him or her off the island.
2. Catch the pickpocket thief and return stolen goods to our guests.
3. Locate where these snakes are coming from and send them home.
4. Rescue Francis and Dakota.
5. Make sure Freddie and his gang never bother any of us again.

"That's my list," she concluded. "Am I missing anything?"

Bernie looked around the group, who all had serious looks on their faces.

"You also need to repair the Magic Portal and figure out what to do with our guests when they learn they can't get off the island," Nathan

Chapter Ten: Everybody Get Ready!

National chimed in. "Which would be right about now."
Stanley Snow spoke up, too. "My fellow Specials, Kate, Robot Guy and me can entertain the guests until the Portal is open again. And we need to tell our guests what the heck is going on. They may not like it, but they need to know the truth."

The rest of Specials nodded their head in agreement.

Gertie piped in too. "I'll go with you and help with any organizing that needs to be done. You can count on me!"

"That's great, everyone," Bernie replied. "I'll work on getting the portal open. We also need Felipe and Frida to provide us with aerial surveillance. We have to find out where the bad guys are hiding. That's where we'll find Francis and Dakota. Finally, after we find the gang and where our friends are located, Aaliya and Nathan will lead the battle against the bad guys."

"We'll get our firefly friends to help search the island," chimed in Frida and Felipe. We'll meet back here lickety-split with our report!"

Everyone nodded their heads thoughtfully in agreement. Aaliya said, "OK, everyone, let's listen to the rest of Bernie's plan and then get to work!"

Bernie quickly brought the group up to date on her research, including the Slumgullion Squad and their profiles, the stinky smells, snakes and lost wallets and watches.

"It looks we're about to have a showdown with the bad guys," said Eileen, her face serious. "There's no one I'd rather be in this fight with than my family and friends."

Joe put his arm around his little but fearless sister. "I'm with you,

Eileen. It's the showdown at Firefly Island. A fight for our home."

"OK everyone, hands in," Nathan said.

They crowded together and put their hands on top of each other in the middle.

"All for one and one for all. Let's win the showdown on Firefly Island!" Nathan shouted.

"Let's goooooo!!" They shouted together and released their hands skyward.

Cookie the dog let go a crazy laugh, "Nyukyukyukiedoodledoo!"

Bernie watched as her friends came together with excitement and confidence to try and turn this tough day around and make it right. You could almost feel and see the good vibrations from the group. She looked up and noticed the sky had brightened. There were still a lot of rainclouds, but here and there, a spot of blue sky. It wasn't a coincidence that teamwork and faith in each other were somehow connected to the weather on Firefly Island. Could she use her theory in the coming fight ahead? We'll soon find out!

Chapter 11:
The Showdown

Everyone headed out to their respective assignments. The Specials hustled down Lulu Lane toward Harmony Lawn, a gathering spot for park guests located next to the portal. Gentle Giant used his booming voice to assemble the park's guests who were converging at the Lawn.

"Everyone, c-can I p-please have your attention. We'd like to explain what's going on."

It was good timing because the guests were wondering where the heck the portal had gone and how they were going to get off the now smelly, snake-y, stealing-y island. It didn't help that an occasional rain cloud was spitting on them, adding insult to injury.

Kate Snow, who wasn't much taller than a munchkin, asked Gentle Giant if he would lift her up so she could talk to the sad-looking crowd. That was easy and before you could say butterscotch, Kate was on GG's shoulder.

In a powerful voice for such a small person, Kate spoke.

"Hello everyone! As we all know, this day of celebration has not turned out the way we all wanted it to, did it? No-siree, Bob, it has not. But the shortest distance between two points is a straight line, or in this case, a straight story. Let me tell you what's happened here today."

And that's precisely what Kate Snow did. She explained all about Francis Fortunato's twin brother Freddie and the Slumgullion squad and why they were making everyone's day miserable. The growing crowd of guests appreciated the honesty and felt bad for Francis, Dakota and the entire Firefly Island clan.

"Don't you worry, folks," she continued. "We're working hard to straighten this out and get you home safe and sound. In the meantime, my friends Gentle Giant and Robot Guy will try and cheer us up with an impromptu performance. But we're going to need your help and participation. Let's hear it for GG and RG!"

There was a smattering of applause as the audience tried to be excited, but they were still bummed out from their day.

Robot Guy stepped forward and took a deep bow. As his feet began to move, it was like the electricity had been turned on at Harmony Lawn. His feet flew and soon, the crowd was smiling and starting to sway in time with the song Step In Time from the musical Mary Poppins. It was a real showstopper.

From behind Robot Guy rose Gentle Giant, who began to pantomime RG's every move. Then he joined in on the song and his beautiful voice soared in harmony with his best friend. Their song filled the air with joy and hope and the audience breathed it in. Kate and Stanley jumped up and joined in. They might be as old as the moon, but boy, they could sure sing and dance! It was a thrilling performance, both sentimental and gorgeous. The crowd stood and cheered and before long, there was dancing everywhere on Harmony Lawn. When Robot Guy found out it was a little girl's birthday, he even led a rousing chorus of Happy Birthday with the entire audience.

Gertie smiled as she watched the Specials give the show of a lifetime and saw the guests' worries and bad moods start to melt away. She rounded up a few of her fellow park workers and had them open up the Sweet Treats store and give all the delicious lunches and desserts out free. Smiles were returning to everyone's faces once again.

Chapter Eleven: The Showdown

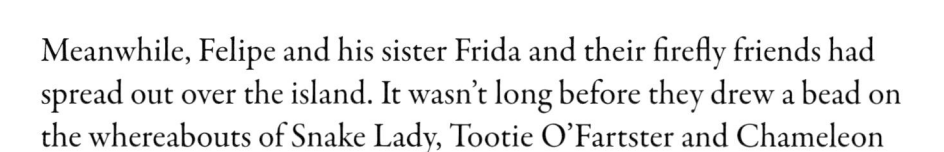

Meanwhile, Felipe and his sister Frida and their firefly friends had spread out over the island. It wasn't long before they drew a bead on the whereabouts of Snake Lady, Tootie O'Fartster and Chameleon Curly.

They had picked up the trail of a whole bunch of snakes slithering in the same direction as Snake Lady, who was painting her fingernails while she waited for her reptile friends to return to her Bag-O-Snakes. Tootie was easy to find. He was hiding under a big tree, but he let a big fart go and it turned a thousand firefly heads. Not to mention the smell as it wafted up in the air. The first firefly in range yelled, "Pee-Yew!" and held his tiny firefly nose.

The firefly patrol duly noted his location and quickly flew away from the smell. Chameleon Curly was tougher to find, given his powers of blending in. But, he had stopped for a minute to count up his stolen cash, jewelry, fit-bits, watches, etc. and one eagle-eye firefly spotted him. While Curly was distracted for a minute, Felipe swooped low and dropped a batch of special pixie dust that settled over his head. He barely noticed the sparkles as he packed up his loot, but now the fireflies could keep an eye on him no matter how much he fit into the scenery. Firefly pixie dust could only be seen by fireflies and from long distances. Curly was soon off in a blur, but he was on their radar now.

Next, a reconnaissance patrol spotted Fast Freddie and Nervous Norvus in the water, looking like they were headed to the Colin Beach, as Bernie had reported. They knew it was Freddie because he was the spitting image of Francis Fortunato, except he had a nasty smile on his face and a Snidely Whiplash handlebar mustache.

The firefly search team still hadn't found Francis and Dakota. Storm clouds with thunderclaps and lightning bolts stopped them from flying over the island's far end where Cauliflower Cove was located.

The bad weather front wasn't moving either. Felipe and Frida thought that was weird because the weather was usually good on the island. But, they had other positive intel to report as they flew into a V formation and skedaddled back to the big oak tree to make their report as fast as their wings could carry them.

"Let's remember to include a weather report in our search update to everyone," Frida shouted to Felipe as they let the wind lift and push them toward their friends.

That turned out to be a good idea.

Chapter 12: The Battle Begins

Felipe and Frida led the firefly reconnaissance team back to the big oak tree. Eileen, Joe and their mom and dad were busy packing provisions: flashlights, their Swiss Army knives, a long coil of rope, maps and other stuff they might need for the upcoming fight to rescue Francis and Dakota. Bernie was working feverishly to rebuild the Magic Portal. She needed to assemble a four-dimensional mathematical calculation capable of mixing just the right amount of particles, dark matter, gravity and little chunks of light that when blended, would result in a new, improved portal. A dash of pixie dust was added for good luck. Of course, it's a lot more complicated than that, but that's why Bernie was a science Brainiac.

Frida and Felipe swooped in low, followed by their fellow scouts, who covered the leaves on the oak tree. Frida reported to the National family the location of each of the Slumgullion squad and the discovery of Freddie and Norvus the Narwhal in the water headed toward Colin's Beach. There was a firefly team assigned to each member of the squad to report any further movement. Now that they knew where their opponents were, they could track them. Nathan and Aaliya were betting wherever the squad was going, they would find Francis and Dakota. But, they didn't know for sure, which bothered them. It was hard to plan a surprise rescue without all of the information.

"One more thing," Felipe said. "Frida noticed there is a storm front over Cauliflower Cove that doesn't seem to be moving. It's the worst weather either of us can remember ever seeing on the island. We can't figure it out, but it sure is strange. The spots of rain and fog we've seen in different parts of the island all day aren't usual either."

That's when the lightbulb lit up for Eileen. "Wait a minute! Bernie has been doing some research on the great weather we have on the island. This might be important, Bernie. Did you hear that report?"

Bernie was stroking her chin, thinking hard. "Yes, I heard it and you're right Eileen, something strange is happening with the weather, ever since the trouble began with Fast Freddie and his gang."

Eileen chimed in, "Bernie has a theory that on Firefly Island, the weather can be predicted by emotions. Happy feelings mean good weather and since there are mostly good times on the island, we have mostly good weather. But when something bad happens, the climate changes, and fast. And there sure has been some terrible stuff going on, with ugly weather to match!"

Bernie agreed. "You're right, Eileen and I'll bet if I look at a recent island weather map, the rain, fog and other bad weather will match up exactly where our firefly friends have tracked the Squad!"

Joe added his two cents worth, too. "I'm not the scientist here, but would that mean where the worst weather is located, might be where we could find Francis and Dakota? Who could be sadder than them?"

"That's it!" Eileen and Bernie exclaimed at the same time.

"Jinx!" yelled Eileen and gently slugged her friend and fellow scientist in the shoulder.

"Well if that's the case, it should be easy to locate Dakota and Francis," Felipe said. "The bad weather has been over Cauliflower Cove since this began. I'll bet that's where the gang first came ashore and where our friends are being held captive. It's trouble doubled by sadness."

Chapter Twelve: The Battle Begins

"Bernie and Eileen, how confident are you that your theory is true? If it is, we can put a rescue plan in action," Aaliya said.

"Let us look at the recent weather maps. It won't take long at all. If they match up, I'm very sure about their location," Bernie replied.

"Me too," agreed Eileen.

"It all makes sense," Nathan mused. "Cauliflower Cove leads right to The Long Forgotten Cavern, the perfect place for a hideout and hostages. It's remote and only accessible by boat, narwhal, or both. That would explain spotting Fast Freddie and the narwhal in the water. And Colin's Beach is on the way to the Cove. Bernie, you and Eileen confirm your findings while Aaliya, Joe and I map out how to chase down the squad and herd them into one place. Most likely the Cove and Cavern."

"You bet. C'mon, Eileen, let's look at this spreadsheet we put together. We'll know in a jiffy." Bernie was confident in her and Eileen's theory. It didn't take long for Aaliya, Nathan and Joe to map out the best strategy to herd the gang into one place. And it didn't take long before Bernie and Eileen confirmed that lousy weather on the island was directly linked to distressing emotions and that wherever the squad members were spotted, miserable weather followed. Most importantly, the worst of it was located right over Cauliflower Cove. When they used their weather app to zoom in, it looked like the mouth of the Long Forgotten Cavern was the center of it all.

That's all the team needed to rush into action. Bernie headed back to the park's entrance to restore the Cloud Portal and the National family jumped in the park's supercharged golf cart to go find the gang. Their educated guess was that with Fast Freddie and Norvus headed towards Colin's Beach, as that was a likely meet-up point. They would encourage their foes to do just that. They could deal with them all there instead of chasing them around the island.

It was a good plan. And Bernie knew one more important piece of the puzzle. If they stayed positive and thought good thoughts, the weather was sure to improve, which could only help them in their quest to find – and free Dakota and Francis and defeat their adversaries.

Already the good weather had returned to Harmony Lawn, where the Specials were still entertaining up a storm. Good feelings were starting to return to Firefly Island.

The National family headed resolutely toward the middle of the island in their souped-up golf cart. They were wearing headbands that matched their belts and were carrying special nun- chucks that could be used, if necessary.

It wasn't long before they found Snake Lady, right where the firefly patrol had spotted her. She was sitting on a fence rail, putting nail polish on her toenails. She was surprised to see them but quickly recovered. She held out her burlap bag of snakes in front of her, which was bulging with her squirming reptiles. A lot of loud hissing was coming out of that bag, too, making it seem downright ominous.

Snake Lady snorted, "Back off you nitwits or I'll unleash all my snakes!"

Eileen stepped forward. "We're not afraid of you or your snakes," she retorted. "In fact, I think your snakes don't much like being cooped up in your dirty old bag. I can't imagine they like working for you. They have three choices: work for you; let us catch them, bag them and take them to the Humane Society; or they could just go home where they came from."

"You're going to be sorry you said that, Missy!" Snake Lady emptied the bag in front of them, covering the ground in front of them with wiggling-waggling snakes.

Chapter Twelve: The Battle Begins

63

Suddenly, the largest snake raised his head and said, "You know, that little girl makes some sense. I'm tired of working for Snake Lady. The pay is terrible and this bag is too small for all of us. Not to mention, we're water snakes and I miss my home on Lake Mucky Ducky. How about it, gang? Let's vamoose!"

The rest of the snakes chimed in.

"Yeah, let's book the heck out of here!"

"I never liked Snake Lady anyway. She's mean."

"She sure is. Let's go!"

Snake Lady snarled, "What do you think you're doing, you good-for-nothing snakes? I have a contract with you. You can't leave!" "Watch us!" the snake leader proclaimed. And with that, the snakes began to slither off together.

Talking snakes was not what the Nationals expected, but they were glad Eileen's speech worked so they didn't have to corral those slippery rascals.

"Hey, the best way to get off the island is to head west to the Colin's Beach," Joe called after the departing snakes. "It's not too far to swim from there to Lake Mucky Ducky."

"Thanks for the tip," answered the biggest snake. "Top of the afternoon to you!"

With that, the snakes made a beeline toward Colin's Beach and wouldn't you know it, they broke into song, singing a popular song with snakes: The Snake by Al Wilson. Those gol-darned snakes boogied right to the water's edge, singing while they slithered.

By the time Eileen, Joe, and Nathan turned around, Snake lady was running as fast as her high heels would take her toward Colin's Beach.

"Great job, Eileen. Offering your opponents a way out is a good way for everyone to win. Except for Snake Lady, of course," Nathan proudly pronounced.

"Thanks, dad. I'm glad it worked because I wasn't looking forward to going on a wild snake chase!"

Joe looked up and saw one of the firefly patrols had formed an arrow in the sky. He pointed up and said, "Looks like Snake Lady is headed to Colin's Beach, just like we hoped. One down, two to go."

Another firefly patrol pointed the National family down Scarlet Street and it didn't take long before they found Chameleon Curly. There was no sign of him at first, but then, they saw a blur and a trail of pixie dust. They were on the right track. Hand-in-hand, the four of them surrounded the pixie dust and closed in. Curly was clever and fast and before they could finally grab him, he had stolen Aaliya's watch, Nathan's bandana, Joe's shoelaces and Eileen's lucky charm bracelet. He was a crazy good thief!

The family finally caught the squirming Curly and Nathan kept a tight hold on him. Nathan patted him on the back and said, "Young man, you are the fastest boy I've ever seen. I bet you could get a track scholarship if you worked and studied hard."

"No way. I'm too stupid. Who would want me in their school?" Curly sneered.

Chapter Twelve: The Battle Begins

Aaliya put her arm around Curly. "That's ridiculous. You're not stupid at all. How else would you still be on the lam and not in jail? You've never been to school, have you?"

"No," Curly scoffed. "School is for losers."

"Curly, I think there's a whole world waiting for you to explore that doesn't involve stealing. If you want to consider leaving this life of crime behind. We can help you with that."

"We'll help you too," Joe said, giving his sister a little nudge. She nodded.

Curly shook his head. "Fiddlesticks!" he said. "No one would ever be that nice to me."

With that, he slipped free and faster than you can say Holy Cow, he was off, straight back to the Long-Forgotten Cavern. "That's OK, let him go. We know where he's going. I don't think Curly is as bad as his reputation," Nathan said. "There's hope for him yet."

Curly took a look back as he scrammed away from the Nationals, muttering to himself, "No one has ever thought I could be a good boy. I wonder…"

The last bad guy on the loose was Tootie O'Fartster. After Fast Freddie, he was the most dangerous member of the Slumgullion Squad. His potions were not only odorific, but could also cast spells, which Francis and Dakota had found out about the hard way.

A firefly patrol led by Felipe flew to the National Family huddle with an update. "We didn't see Tootie because he was smart enough to stay under the cover of the trees," he reported. "But we could smell him and he headed toward Colin's Beach. That's where all three of them are headed.

"Thanks, Felipe. That's very helpful. It's time for Phase II of our plan," Aaliya said.

Felipe gave a crisp salute with one of his four wings and was on his way.

Right then, a series of shrill whistles filled the air. It was the Squad calling out for Norvus to pick them up. Before long, a firefly patrol reported back on the transport of the gang by Norvus to Cauliflower Cove and the Long-Forgotten Cavern.

"OK, we have the Squad in one place," Nathan told the National clan. "Fast Freddie will be trying to contact us soon with directions on how to turn the park over to him. We need to surprise them before that. Are you ready?"

"Yes!" the National family said in unison, Cookie joining in with "Yippee!"

Back near the park's entrance, Bernie was working feverishly to fix the Magic Portal.

Kate and Stanley Snow, Robot Guy and Gentle Giant kept the guests' minds off their troubles by continuing their entertainment, now with calming songs. Gertie made sure everyone had enough food and drinks and knew the locations of the bathrooms.

The National family was readying for battle.

Meanwhile, Freddie Fortunato and the Slumgullion Squad were making their own plans.

There was a showdown brewing on Firefly Island. And even though the sky was clearing over much of the island, behind Snow Mountain, where Cauliflower Cove led to the Long-Forgotten Cavern, the sky was turning an ugly black and green and the deep rumble of thunder growled and vibrated like a herd of wild animals stampeding.

What was going to happen next?

We can't wait to find out!

Chapter 13: Nuts!

The National family was confident they could defeat Fast Freddie and his gang and rescue Francis and Dakota. They had already eliminated Snake Lady's snakes and had a feeling that Chameleon Curly's heart might not be in the fight. But they knew that the formidable Freddie and the Slumgullion Squad would fight dirty. They needed the element of surprise to win the day.

That's where the Secrets of Firefly Island book came into play. Dakota's grandmother had written the book. It laid out the island's history and how her ancestors had successfully lived there for generations, farming and trading. It was a peaceful life until the appearance of pirates from across the sea. The secrets in the book included many hidden passageways and hideouts on the island that Dakota's ancestors had built to protect themselves in case of just such an invasion.

It described how the invaders had attacked the island from boats filled with the snarky pirates. The pirates thought it would be an easy fight to win because it was a small island without many warriors to defend it. They didn't know about the secret hiding places which had many more fighters than the invaders expected. Because Firefly Island was their home, everyone, old and young, chipped in to repel the attackers.

As the pirate attack began, the islanders appeared out of nowhere from their hiding places and yelled, "Nuts to You!" and, "Nuts Ahoy!"

Suddenly, the air was filled with objects flying toward the invaders. It was a hailstorm of nuts, black walnuts and shagbark hickory nuts, to be specific. The islanders had built slingshots and catapults just for this purpose and were experts at slinging. It was raining nuts down on the bad guys and those big kernels stung like crazy!

Even worse, the black walnuts had green hulls which left a nasty stain that took forever to wash out. The invaders beat a hasty retreat and headed home, defeated. They were covered from head to toe with red marks and green stains from the nuts hitting their targets. Since they didn't like a fair fight, they never returned.

Through the years, the victory story became known as The Battle of the Nuts. The news traveled far and wide and anyone who wanted to take over Firefly Island knew they were in for a tough fight. As a result, the islanders lived in peace for generations.

No one had used the secret hiding places and passageways for a long time, but they were still there. When Dakota was a child, her grandmother and mother had taken her for long hikes, visiting all of the secret nooks, crannies and caves. She knew them all like the back of her hand.

Dakota had no children of her own to share the secrets with, so she had confided in Aaliya and taken her on the same trails she had learned as a child. Only a few short months ago, she had given the book to Aaliya.

"Aaliya, even though I don't have a daughter, I think of you like one," she said. "Here is my most precious possession. The Firefly Island Book of Secrets. Let this book be part of your life with your family on the island."

This brought tears to Aaliya's eyes and she hugged Dakota. "I love you, Dakota and I'm proud to be your daughter. I will honor you and the Islanders' legacy and teach my children and grandchildren all about your ancestors and the history of your island home.

Dakota knew the map in the book could give her family and friends the advantage they needed to defeat Fast Freddie. Now she spread out the map and pointed to the Long-Forgotten Cavern.

"Based on Bernie and Eileen's information, this is where we'll find them," she said. "We can surprise the gang from four different directions if we use the secret tunnels."

She pointed to a path just outside Snow Mountain that led into the tunnels. From there, they would follow separate tunnels to four secret doors that opened up into the back of the Cavern.

"If we're quiet and careful, they will never hear us coming," Nathan piped up. "There's a chance we can sneak Francis and Dakota out of the Cavern without being noticed. If discovered, we have the element of surprise – and plenty of ammunition!"

The land near Snow Mountain was filled with shagbark hickory and black walnut trees loaded with nuts and the Nationals had brought bags to collect them. Nuts had won the battle once before at Firefly Island and the Nationals were counting on history repeating itself.

With their plans in place, they hopped in their golf cart. With Nathan driving, Aaliya, Joe, Eileen and Cookie pointed towards Snow Mountain, ready to fight for their friends – and themselves!

They passed by the Truly Scrumptious Toboggan Ride and turned the corner toward a dead end, where they parked before tiptoeing down a barely visible path toward the super-secret entrance. On the way, they filled their sacks and backpacks with the nuts that were lying everywhere on the ground. With full sacks, they were ready to rumble.

"OK kids, once we get inside, you take the paths to the far left and

Chapter Thirteen: Nuts!

right," Nathan whispered. "When you get to the end, open the door just a smidge and sneak a peek across the cave. If you see a thumbs up, it's game time. We'll sneak up and see if we can free Francis and Dakota and take them back the way we came in. If something goes wrong, run back to your tunnel and let those nuts fly!"

Aaliya chimed in. "If we can't push back the gang, I want you kids to promise me that if I tell you to scram, you'll scram! Run back to the tunnel and the golf cart and head back to Harmony Lawn. Bernie and Gertie will be there to figure out how to get help. OK?"

"OK mom," Eileen replied. "But we're going to make this work."

Joe gave a thumbs up.

"Alright then, let's get this party started!" Nathan said.

The National family put on their headlamps, turned them on and opened the door that led to the four secret tunnels. They followed their individual paths, with Cookie trailing behind Eileen. The tunnels wound in a circle and it wasn't long before each of the hidden doors opened up, just a smidge. Aaliya stuck her hand through the opening and gave a thumbs up signal. All four of the Nationals turned their headlamps off and slowly, ever so quietly emerged into the dim light at the very back of the Long-Forgotten Cavern. So far, so good! A few steps later, they could see in the shadows what they hoped for – Francis and Dakota sitting on the cave floor, fast asleep.

The four rescuers quietly crept closer and closer to their sleeping friends. There wasn't any sign of Freddie and his pals, probably because they didn't know about the back doors. They edged forward, step by step, inch by inch, close enough to reach and touch their friends. Then all heck broke loose!

A bright light switched on, temporarily blinding the Nationals. They shielded their eyes to see, but it was too late! Freddie and Snake lady tossed a heavy net at them. It landed right on top of the family and they struggled to get free.

Horror of horrors: before they could pull the net away, a sickening, sweet smell was upon them. The Scoundrel of Stink, Tootie O'Fartster, was blowing a devilish cloud in their direction.

The Nationals tried to hold their breath, but the stinky mist was a sleeping potion. A few seconds later, they fell into a deep sleep.

In in the chaos of the moment, no one noticed that Cookie had snuck under the net. Tootie didn't know the sleeping potion didn't work on dogs!

"Hey, that laughing dog is getting away!" Curly shouted.

"Don't worry about it, Curly. What's a stupid dog going to do? Who does he think he is, Lassie?" Freddie laughed loudly. The Slumgullion Squad joined in the laughter.

"I knew the Nationals wouldn't follow my orders, although I must admit, I didn't expect them to come through the back of the cave," Freddie said. "Good thing Norvus has a nose for strangers! Now we've got them right where we want them. When they wake up, Francis, Dakota, Nathan and Aaliya will sign the contracts giving up the park–or else! The time of reckoning is near!"

Cookie the laughing dog wasn't laughing. He was already out of the tunnel and running like a greyhound, picking up speed with every lope. He knew what he had to do and nothing was going to get in his way. Next stop: Harmony Lawn.

Chapter 14:
Bernie to the Rescue

Meanwhile, back at Harmony Lawn, Robot Guy and Gentle Giant had brought the crowd to their feet with their rousing George M. Cohan medley of Yankee Doodle Dandy/Grand Old Flag/Give My Regards to Broadway followed by Woodie Guthrie's This Land is Your Land.

Robot Guy asked the crowd to quiet down and spoke up. "Thank you so much for being such a great audience. We're so happy to see the smiles on your faces. But, as Mrs. Snow told you, some bad folks are trying to take the park away from the Fortunato's, and if you think about it, from all of us who get to perform and work here and really, you too!"

Gentle Giant, while a wonderful performer, chimed in. "Th-that's t-t-true. We l-love Fran-cis and Dakota!"

GG had tears in his eyes and the crowd could feel the emotion. A small little girl in a yellow dress called out. "Hey, what can we do to help?"

That brought out other shouts from the audience.

"Yeah, we want to help!"

"We can't let those scalawags get away with taking our park!"

No one really knew what a scalawag was, but the crowd got the general idea.

Just then, there was a loud CRAAAACK!! Followed by a POOF! A cloud of fog settled over Firefly Island until a sudden gust of wind blew the mist away. The Magic Cloud Portal had reappeared, right back where it belonged!

Out of the haze, Bernie appeared with what looked like a Ghostbusters proton pack. But, Bernie's contraption didn't zap ghosts, it rebuilt a portal.

"I fixed the Portal and found a way to make it portable!" Bernie reported.

"Hurray for Bernie!" the crowd bellowed.

Bernie smiled shyly and bowed her head slightly.

"Thanks, everyone. The Magic Cloud Portal is back in business and better than ever, with exceptional protection in place so a bad guy like Freddie can never disable it again. If our guests want to go cross through the portal to return to the village and their cars, all systems are A-OK."

A teenage boy stood up and said, "We need to help take the park back first. Are you with me, everyone!" The guests cheered wildly.

Right on cue, Cookie scooted into Harmony Lawn and, seeing Bernie, screeched to a stop right in front of her, panting so heavily, his tongue touched the ground.

"Cookie, what are you doing here?" Bernie asked. "I thought you were with the Nationals?"

Cookie dropped the map, took a deep breath and then started yipping and pantomiming the story that the Nationals were in

Chapter Fourteen: Bernie to the Rescue

trouble, their plan had failed, and they were being held hostage along with Dakota and Francis. In other words, disaster!

Fortunately, Cookie was an excellent pantomimer, learned by playing charades with the National family. It also helped that Bernie was his friend and understood him. It was even better when Bernie picked up the map showing the secret tunnels.

Bernie turned to the assembled crowd. "Friends, the National family bravely tried to rescue Francis and Dakota but were foiled by sleeping gas," she explained. "Now they are all in the hands of the bandits. If we all show up, it will be too many people for Fast Freddie and the Slumgullions to handle."

As Bernie held up the map, the entire swarm of millions of fireflies appeared over the horizon. Frida and Felipe settled on each of Gentle Giant's shoulders.

"We're in this fight with you," Felipe announced. "We'll fly around to the front of the Long-Forgotten Cavern and do our best to confuse those no-good varmints!"

A cheer went up from the crowd. Then Bernie explained to the crowd in the shortest way she could that if they all thought good, positive thoughts, it could only help their cause. She figured trying to explain the weather connection was too complicated. But, if the group were upbeat, maybe, just maybe, the bad storms over the Cove and near Snow Mountain would calm down, making their battle more likely to succeed.

Then, a tiny figure appeared on the Harmony Lawn stage. It was grandma Gertie.

"Excuse me, Bernie, but can that newfangled portal squirt gun make a path through a mountain?" Gertie asked.

Bernie laughed out loud. "You're right, grandma. What a brilliant idea! I can open a portal right into the Long-Forgotten Cavern. We can march right in!"

"Let's go!" The crowd went bananas!

She held up the giant squirt gun over her head and started to march down Asher Lane toward Snow Mountain. Her friends Robot Guy, Gentle Giant, Kate and Stanley Snow joined in right behind her, followed by one thousand guests. A gorgeous swarm of fireflies flew overhead. It was just turning dusk and their tiny blinkers were starting to brighten, which was a real sight to behold. Bringing up the rear was grandma Gertie, tapping her cane as she went. They were on a mission to bring All the Fun Under the Sun back to their park.

Fast Freddie was in for a big surprise!

Chapter 15:
All Bad Things Must Come to an End

After the group reached Snow Mountain, Bernie wisely assessed that they needed to spread out to take advantage of their numbers.

Like a general, she dispatched hundreds of guests to fan out across the mountain and nearby, to prevent a surprise escape. She asked for volunteers to scurry through the tunnels on the map and be ready to open the secret door when she gave the signal. She then arranged the guests in rows of four that could rush through the portable portal when she started it up.

Bernie looked over the assembled group and gave Gentle Giant a thumbs up. GG's powerful baritone voice was better than a loudspeaker and would announce to everyone to begin the battle. Gentle Giant and Robot Guy were singers and dancers, not used to a fight, but they were ready to use their special skill anyway they could to help win the day.

The fireflies were hovering over Snow Mountain, ready to keep an eye on everything around the Long-Forgotten Cavern once the battle began. Bernie pointed the portable portal contraption at the mountain, right at the Long-Forgotten Cavern, and fired! A low rumble began, followed by a CRACKKK! A mist appeared instantaneously and created a magical tunnel big enough for the charge.

"Let's go!" Bernie shouted.

That was GG's signal.

"CHAAARGE!"

Everyone pushed forward with the battle cry on their lips. It was quite a sight to see the enthusiastic guests, with determined looks on their faces moving shoulder-to-shoulder toward, well, they weren't sure exactly what they would find. But, they knew there was strength in numbers and there were a lot of them, which helped their confidence. That, and Bernie, in her nerdy way, was showing a lot of courage and leadership.

"CHAAARGE!"

And charge they did.

Chapter Fifteen: All Bad Things Must Come to an End

At the same time, Fast Freddie Fortunato and the Slumgullion Squad were enjoying their success so far. The chaos they created at the park had ruined the big day. They had nabbed Dakota and Francis and beat back the surprise raid by the National family. Fast Freddie toasted their achievements with hot chocolate just as Dakota, Francis and the National family were waking up from their stinky slumber. All they had left to do was force their captives to sign over the park to Freddie, boot them off the island and their goals would be reached. They had no idea that they were celebrating too soon.

The magic portal opened up at the same time as the secret doors and the Firefly Island army poured through into the Long-Forgotten Cavern.

Freddie and the squad were caught entirely by surprise. Snake Lake opened her mouth to scream, but no sound came out. Nervous Norvus looked like he was going to cry. Fast Freddie shouted a word that can't be repeated in a children's book.

Curly's jaw dropped and grunted, "This doesn't look good."

Tootie grabbed for his stinky sleep potion. But the secret door soldiers emerged with the bags of nuts left behind by the National family and started pelting the squad, starting with Tootie.

"Ouchie, that smarts! Cut that out!" Tootie retreated away from his bag of smelly tricks, his skin covered with a green stain from the shagbark hickory nuts.

Snake Lady and Chameleon Curly, too stunned to move at first, quickly recovered and beat a hasty retreat toward the mouth of the Cavern.

"Not so fast, buckaroos," said Robot Guy, who used his fast dancing skills to quick-step and cha-cha his way in front of the super-fast Curly and super-slippery Snake Lady could make an exit.

"Drat, you dancing rat!" Snake lady snarled.

"Hey, how'd you get there, you...you...robot!" Curly spluttered.

The name-calling didn't last long

"Hey, you bandoleros, take this!" Kate and Stanley stepped forward and began heaving a rainbow of snow cone snowballs they had brought with them from their attraction.

A red and yellow one-hit Snake Lady right smack dab in the neck and she started to cry. "Owie, owie, zowie, I've been hit and it smarts. I want my mommy!"

A green and pink snowball hit Curly right on his chameleon bootie. He screamed like a banshee. "Ay caramba, you got me!"

While they were getting pummeled, they discovered that the snowballs were darn tasty! "Ouch, that hurts, but yum – blueberry!" Curly exclaimed.

Both Snake Lady and Curly sat down and began licking their snow cone snowballs. Tootie cowered with his hands over his head. He was sick of getting pelted with nuts. Kate and Stanley and Robot Guy surrounded them, so they didn't cause any more trouble. These three were out of the battle. That left only Nervous Norvus and Fast Freddie. Norvus looked confused, not quite sure whether to fight or flee. Stanley tossed his last snowball which smacked the narwhal.

"Ouch!" Cried the startled Norvus. While his thick layer of blubber cushioned the blow, his feelings were hurt, and he slinked away, also out of the fight.

Chapter Fifteen: All Bad Things Must Come to an End   81

Freddie saw what was happening and knew that the battle was lost. In all the excitement, he tiptoed unnoticed in the shadows toward the cave entrance. Norvus was already in the water, getting ready for a water escape, Freddie ran up beside him and jumped on his back. "Cheese it, Norvus, we need to scramola out of here!"

OUCHHH!!!

Norvus, who was nervous anyway, hightailed it away from the Cove at top speed with Freddie holding on tight. But before you could say Rumpelstiltskin, a parade of fireflies was buzzing all around them. Norvus started to shake, rattle and roll to keep the tiny little lights away from his eyes. Freddie was waving his arms back and forth, trying to keep his balance. As Norvus bucked, Freddie sailed into the air and splashed into the water.

Fast Freddie, who didn't know how to swim, began flailing back and forth. It didn't look good for him. Then, out of nowhere, he was lifted from the water – by Gentle Giant! He plucked Freddie out of the soup by his collar with this thumb and pointer finger.

GG was too big to go through the portable portal or the tunnels, so he'd decided to climb down the back of Snow Mountain. He arrived just in time to stop Freddie from escaping and save his life to boot! There was a very large table rock at the cavern's entrance and GG deposited Freddie on it and shooed Nervous Norvus near the shore too.

It was crowded inside the cavern and Dakota, Francis and the Nationals were still a little woozy as they shook off the effects of the sleep potion. Bernie, Robot Guy, Kate and Stanley Snow all lent their shoulders to help their friends out of the cavern and into the fresh air of Cauliflower Cove. The crowd ushered Snake Lady, Curly and Tootie onto the big rock with Freddie and Norvus. The gang hung their heads in defeat. Francis Fortunato took a deep breath of the fresh sea air, linked arms with Dakota and addressed the crowd.

"First of all, I want to thank all of you, from the bottom of my heart, for coming to rescue my family and friends. It was courageous and we'll never forget what you did for all of us. I suppose even though the big celebration didn't go as planned, it will still be a day to remember and I promise we'll find a way to pay you back."
Eileen stepped forward and raised her hand in the air. "Here's to everyone who fought at the Showdown at Firefly Island. Hip-hip-hooray!"

The crowd joined in, raising their hands and voices. "HIP-HIP-HOORAY!"

"Freddie, my long-lost twin brother," Francis continued. "How could our lives come to this where we are enemies? Life is too short for hate and fighting. At our age, we need to focus on QTR: Quality Time Remaining. We shouldn't spend a minute on anything that doesn't bring us peace. I know I should be angry with you, but I'm just sad. What are we going to do with you?"

Firefly Frida was hovering just off the big rock where the gang stood.

"I know a place that's between hither and yon that would give your brother some time to think about starting a new life," she piped up. "It's where our firefly brothers and sisters go on vacation. We can keep an eye on Freddie and he can help us with our garden and other chores. What do you think, Francis?"

Chapter Fifteen: All Bad Things Must Come to an End

"That's a grand idea, Frida! It's very generous of you and your friends."

Francis turned to his brother. "Maybe after some time, Freddie, you can come back and we can try to patch things up between us. I have missed you all these years, and I still love you, brother," Francis said, with tears collecting in his eyes.

That caught Freddie by surprise. He was expecting a much worse reaction. At first, he pushed back a bit.

"Looks like I don't have any choice," Freddie grumbled and shuffled his feet. "I'm not sure why you're being so nice to me. I tried to ruin your life." "Once a twin brother, always a twin brother, Freddie."

"I don't know what to say, brother. I'm not sure I remember how to be good anymore. But, I guess I could give your firefly vacation spot a try." Freddie said quietly.

"That sounds like a yes. OK, Frida, how do you transport my brother?

"That's simple. Felipe will lead the way!"

With that, all of the assembled fireflies formed a posse and swooped over Freddie. Frida directed her firefly friends like the maestro of an orchestra and the sparkling fireflies moved in unison, lifting Freddie up into a firefly hammock. As they rose, a peaceful grin came over Freddie's face. The firefly hammock had a way of bringing out the best in a person, even Fast Freddie Fortunato.

As he passed by his brother and the rest of the crowd, he called out, "Francis, this feels great–so warm and fun! Like when we used to turn double plays. Oh, I miss those days. I miss you, Francis. Can I come back soon?" He choked up and tears filled his eyes. "And can we start being brothers again?"

Tears rolled down Francis's cheek as he called out, "Yes, Freddie. Yes! Let's be brothers again! And we can have a game of catch when you get back. There's a high school team that needs a coach. We could do it together!"

A full moon rose as the sun set. On the left, the moon reflected its shimmering whiteness across the sea. On the right, the setting sun's red orb bounced yellow, orange and pink rays off the water, meeting the moonbeams. There was nary a cloud in the sky, and it was a sight to behold. Trouble was leaving Firefly Island and good times and sunny weather had returned.

Francis put his head on Dakota's shoulder and watched as his brother flew away as if he was lifted by the hand of God. The twinkling of the fireflies mimicked the first stars of night as they disappeared over the horizon.

Cookie let out a barking laugh. Everyone laughed along and there were hugs and high fives all around. Tears and laughter seemed a fitting end to a remarkable day.

Denouement

After the battle, everyone returned to Harmony lawn, feeling pretty darn good. The National family stepped onto the stage and Francis thanked the happy crowd.

"From the bottom of my heart, you all mean so much to me," he said. "I can never repay you, but I hope you know how much we love you all. It's with great pride that at the end of this momentous day, we turn the keys and the park's future over to Aaliyah and Nathan National and their family. It's all yours now!"

The National family hugged each other. Their dream had come true. The crowd cheered as Aaliya moved to the front and asked for quiet.

"We're so grateful for everything our friends and mentors have done for our family, our fellow park associates and all of you," she said. "We've talked it over as a family and decided that after today, we are asking Bernie and all the Specials to join us as owners. Together, we'll continue to follow the example of Francis and Dakota. And from now on, for every ticket we sell, we'll donate to the Dakota Leelanau and Francis Fortunato Scholarship Fund. We'd like Bernie's grandma Gertie to be the Fund President, to make sure anyone that wants a college education gets one!"

Well, that blew the roof off and the crowd cheered wildly. They ushered Gertie to the front and as she took a bow, even though she was as old as the hills, she skipped backward, just like she was a kid again. That set off a spontaneous celebration that might still be happening today, except that children were beginning to yawn.

There was one more item to wrap up on this story. What happened to the Slumgullion Squad? As it turns out, if given a gentle nudge in the right direction, even the meanest, worst villains can change.

The first thing the Specials did was make Tootie O'Fartster take a long shower. When he emerged, clean for the first time in who-knows-how-long, he found out he liked the minty fresh smell and tingly feeling of Dr. Bronner's peppermint soap. Kate and Stanley Snow took him under their wing, finding out his real name was Danny O'Dublin. They also found out he was lactose intolerant, which was one reason he was a walking flatus factory. He had to give up his favorite beverage, chocolate milk, but it was worth it to stop the nonstop tooting.

It also turned out Tootie had a knack for making fantastic flavors they could add to the snow cone slushies at the Truly Scrumptious Toboggan Ride. That's where he works today; making children happy. He's become great friends with Kate and Stanley Snow. Of course, every once in a while, he still farts a little. Who doesn't?

Snake Lady was very sad and felt lost without her snakes, thinking she had no future. Robot Guy and Gentle Giant discovered she had grown up learning to play the harp and was quite good at it. She stopped playing when her life of reptilian crime started.

It just so happens that Robot Guy and GG had an old harp at their Emporium. They cleaned and polished it up, presenting it to her as a gift. She had tears in her eyes because it was the first present she had been given in a very long time. After practicing for hours every day, it wasn't long before she was on stage with Gentle Giant and Robot Guy. Her real name was Melody Glissandro, a much better stage name than Snake Lady! Melody can be found every day working with her new best friends, Robot Guy and Gentle Giant. Their trio has become a crowd favorite. Funny how things work out, isn't it?

That rascal Chameleon Curly reformed his ways, too. Hidden beneath his tough-guy swagger was a gentle soul. With a lot of encouragement from the National family and Bernie, he blossomed into a fine young man and became the first recipient of the Dakota and Francis Scholarship, awarded by grandma Gertie. Instead of using his speed for stealthy stealing, Curly became a track star, winning many 100-meter dashes. When he wasn't away at college, he lived with Bernie and Gertie, his new family.

It wasn't long before Freddie Fortunato returned to Firefly Island a changed man. He moved in with Dakota and Francis until he designed his own unique house, which he built in a nearby tree. After so many years apart, they were now neighbors. The brothers became coaches of the Village of Billrita's high school baseball team and won a championship. There's a picture on Freddie's fireplace mantel of him and Francis holding up the trophy their team won.

After all that excitement, everyone was ready to get back into their regular routine. But they also made a new tradition. Once a week, all the staff at the park, the National family, Gertie, Bernie, the Specials, Francis, Freddie and Dakota and the former Slumgullion Gang meet at Harmony Lawn for a sing-along. Even Cookie barks along laughingly! For the last song, they all link arms and start to sway in time. The song reminds them of where they came from and how fortunate they are to have each other as friends and family. Grateful and at peace, they sing to their heart's content.

> Oh we ain't got a barrel of money
> Maybe we're ragged and funny
> But we'll travel along
> Singing a song
> Side by side
>
> We don't know what's a-comin' tomorrow
> Maybe it's trouble and sorrow
> But we'll travel the road
> Sharing our load
> Side by side
>
> When they've all had their quarrels and parted
> We'll be the same as we started
> Just a traveling along
> Singing a song
> Side by side!

That would end another day on Firefly Island Park of Wonders where everyone did their best to have all the fun under the sun and usually succeeded.

Acknowledgements

Many thanks to the Detroit Writing Room (www.detroitwritingroom.com) for providing resources for our book, including Lizz Schumer, who edited our book. The DWR provide outstanding services of all kinds to writers.

Kudos to My Book Printer (www.MyBookPrinter.com) who printed our book and much more. A lot of little touches made a big difference.

Thank you to our families for their story telling ideas and to Mom/Moira and Kathy/Grandma for their ideas and pushing us to get it done right!